THE
SIEGE
OF
HARLEM

Books by Warren Miller

The Sleep of Reason
The Way We Live Now
The Cool World
90 Miles from Home
Flush Times
Looking for the General
The Siege of Harlem

THE
SIEGE
OF
HARLEM

by Warren Miller

MC GRAW-HILL BOOK COMPANY
New York   Toronto   London

for Gita and Marshall

How cometh joy to a man of hating
that he hath one time loved or of
bearing wrath and hate toward that
therein he had one time set his
heart? What he hath loved he ought
not hate, but he may well depart
and remove him when he seeth
therein no cause to love.
                    —*The Romance of Tristram & Ysolt*

". . . en den dey bo'd little holes
in de groun' en went down outer
sight."
        "Who did, Uncle Remus?" asked
the little boy.
        "De Crawfishes, honey. Dey
bo'd inter de groun' en kep' on
bo'in twel dey onloost de fountains
er de earf; en de waters squirt
out, en riz higher en higher twel
de hills wuz kivvered, en de
creeturs wuz all drownded; en all
bekaze dey let on 'mong deyselves
dat dey wuz bigger dan
de Crawfishes."
        —The Story of the Deluge, from *Uncle Remus*

ONE

Get your hand out of my pocket and your feet off my back!" the old gentleman said. "That is what we told them, if not in so many words, which they would not do. Then we presented the bill and they would not pay it. We had tried every which way to collect on the promise. Due date had come and gone not once but a hundred times. We demanded payment from the Privileged People, but they would not pay."

"Where were you then, Grandpa?" little Ngomo asked.

"I'll get to that bimeby, honey," the old man said. He filled his pipe, and with slow movements lighted it and brushed flakes of tobacco from his lap. The children, accustomed to his ways, waited patiently.

The old man said, "I will now pursue the tale of the most significant occasion I have ever seen in the history of the world, which was the day that Harlem turned a blind face to the city of New York and originated itself as one of the great black capitals of this earth."

"Where were you then, Grandpa?"

"Didn't I already tell you about that, honey? Well, just prior to the time that Lance Huggins put out his famous call and called the children home, I was living in the place of my birth, dear old Smudgeville, Georgia. I was born uptown on Snade Street, near the bridge; was Baptist from birth and had friends for miles around. So now you know all about where I was just prior."

"I had become the age of fifteen years old," Mboya said.

"I had become the age of fifteen years old when I received the call, down there in dear old Smudgeville. Yes, because my birthday is somewhere in March. I was good to go as soon as I heard the call and I heard it soon enough for it was the town's talk."

Sekou, one of the older children, whispered to his brother, "Huggins! Snade! Smudgeville! The *names, my dear. Quel mauvais ton.*"

The old gentleman stopped rocking and leaned forward. "Boy, you are being monstrous sly," he said; then sat back and folded his hands around his pipe. "I'm not telling any more tales to bad children."

Sekou apologized.

"Go on with the tale, please," Mboya said, stroking his grandfather's hand.

The old gentleman said to Sekou, "You're not mad at me, are you, honey?—All right, then. What I tell you when I first begin? I told you that Lance Huggins sent out the call and all those that could, from Alabama, Georgia, New Orleans and other of the dear old states, came home. Lance Huggins' call was a masterpiece. It was at that time the greatest in existence as I can remember.

"Following the strict and legal ways, Lance Huggins said, taking all those measures under the law which are available to us, seeking equality and happiness and in pursuit of that which is our birthright, knocking on the doors of lots of people in the White House and other residences, and being met with the show of good will and actions which are indifferent and even less, we got now no other recourse, no other recourse."

"Oh my," little Ngomo said.

"Yes, honey, it was a sad sad situation for anyone to witness. The Majority People just would not turn go of us. Lance said, he said, We got a long way to go and a short time to make it in. Well, there was a lot more to the call than that. I'm just trying to give you a fast picture of it. It didn't have a lot of that swell ta-doo stuff they put in nowadays," the old man said, looking at Sekou. "Verbally speaking, that is."

The old gentleman waited for a respectful silence and then continued. "I will now pursue the tale. Bimeby, in various small places hardly on the map and where the Greyhound never stopped, we received the call and many thousands strong we started out, some walking, some riding the trains and buses, all of us young and willing and with a purpose. Many fast friendships were made while on the road and all our talk alluded to Harlem and Lance Huggins, former U.S. Congressman.

"The shape that I was in at that time I could walk all night and way up in the day. So we all could and what's more did, meanwhile hitching rides in potato trucks and such with cooperating brothers. We were handed from willing hand to willing hand all the way, and it was just the other side of dear old Baltimore, on a road bordered with blossoming trees of one kind of fruit or another—maybe it was apples, maybe it was cherries—that I met your sainted grandmother, a girl of twelve years old at this time of which I am now telling, and dedicated to freedom."

"Inshallah," little Shabad said in a voice full of feeling.

"She was a Baptist too, I am happy to relate," the old man said. "Although I do believe we are all one in the sight of God if we are black. Now where was I?"

"Outside Baltimore."

"Tooby sure, honey. Outside Baltimore was where we met a man named Hatrack Johnson—I don't want to hear any commentaries!—an ice cream salesman who had also received the call. He piled eight of us youngsters, including in this eight your grand-mother and me, into his Buick automobile and we drove together in high style and comfort to what was then still 125th Street and is now known as Huggins Boulevard.

"Where we were welcomed in our thousands by Lance himself. You would have witnessed a lot of joyous expressions on that day, dearies. Lance said,

We have not seen the like of such a manifestation since the ancient days of the Children's Crusade. And he went on in that vein. Once Lance got the slite of something, boy, he really went and it was a wonder to the ears.

"Night fell on us suddenly and we were still standing there in good old Harlem Plaza and all of a sudden the lights went on, up and down every street in view. I tell you, I was stunned; for living all my life hitherto in Smudgeville I had never in all my history seen so many lights. Never will I forget it. I took hold of the hand of your sainted and stood there stunned by the magnificent display."

"Didn't they have any lights in dear old Smudge-ville, Grandpa?"

"Very little, honey. Now where was I at?"

"In what was then Harlem Plaza," Jomo said.

"All right then. Well, it so transpired, as I only then discovered, that we were the last contingent to arrive before the deed was done and we all moved rapidly to our assigned tasks."

"With sly and cunning hands," Mboya said.

"With sly and cunning hands we boarded over the windows of Harlem's north and south frontiers, on 97th Street looking downtown and on 145th Street looking uptown, from river to river; and we raised barriers across every street, consisting of abandoned automobiles, mattresses, orange crates, and such like, until by morning the heart of Harlem was sealed and we had turned a blind face to those who had turned always hitherto a blind face to us.

"Now unless I'm running into some mistakes, the wee morning hours came upon me as I was putting some artful finishing touches to a tank trap at the corner of Fifth Avenue and 97th Street. Yes, children, this is the first dawn in the new history of Harlem and though many years have flowed since that auspicious day, there isn't the least significant detail which I don't remember.

"It was the day we began to make our own history, all other means legal and agitational having failed. No other recourse remained, as Lance said. We had broken loose at last.

"I put out for home, which was at that time the famous Hotel Theresa where I was billeted as it is called, and which had that day become the temporary Black House for Lance Huggins and his staff. It was as pretty a morning as you can imagine and all our streets looked spruce and new. The dawn was green, it reminded me of back home. There was a Muslim on a rooftop calling his people to prayer . . ."

"May His Name be praised," Shabad murmured.

". . . and in front of the Bookstore of Proper Propaganda there are two white policemen who do not yet know that this is their last hour in Harlem. They were all soon thereafter escorted to the border and frozen out."

"Oh my," little Ngomo said.

"Yes, honey, it was a historical occasion of joy and sadness mixed; and there was dancing in streets, true, but also wringing of the hands for no one *wants* to be separate."

"What about Lance and Miss Brindle?"

"I'm not up to that part yet, honey. I will tackle it later on, for right now I have to cut out for the monthly meeting of The Veterans of the First Day Lodge. As you know, I am one of a certified three who is still casting a shadow."

"What about Art Rustram?"

"I will tell you all about that another day if you are good children. I'll bring you up to date on all the most significant events of Harlem's first year, but it is your bedtime now, honey."

TWO

Well, children, the siege of Harlem was on; and the eyes of the world were focused upon us. Because when it comes to moral force, Lance said, then this Harlem is the spiritual capital of the world. Lance said, We have been inspired to take the national cancer and localize it for all to see."

"It was a mixed situation of danger and opportunity both," Mboya said.

"That's exactly what it was, honey. Now you're talking. It was a mixed situation all right and there were a lot of outside people trying in every kind of way to put an end to it. But we countered their cunning with cunning of our own and we had a lot of good friends in the international picture down at the U.N. It was on account of outraging this opinion, Lance said, that they did not move the federal troops against us; although, tooby sure, on the second day there they were, lined up all along both sides of the

15

demarcation. They said they were up here to protect Washington Heights and Manhattan, thinking we were going to raid them, poor souls, I guess. But we never *had* anything in those two places, and we were not inspired to do what we had done in order to take what was not rightly ours."

"Meanwhile, Miss Brindle was still in Teaneck, New Jersey, I guess," Jomo said.

"I'm about to project that story, honey, but I'd just like to pause and pay tribute to our brave militia, which included your dear grandmother. They faced the soldiers of the Privileged People all along the line and never once flinched and never one of them went over to the other side, though tempting offers were made at all times—a free trip to Miami; a color teevee set; a complete set of forty copper-bottomed pots and pans; an electric swizzle stick; a lifetime subscription to *House & Garden* magazine—and though there was ample talk in their newspapers about people voting with their feet and all. Maybe there were a few for there is always some, but not one solitary voter came from our militia.

"My but the rumors were thick and strong in those early days of Harlem. Hardly an hour pass but what we did not hear something, such as that an army was being raised against us down in Mobile, in Atlanta, in Birmingham, and in various other antique cities of that nature, with brigades named in memory of their most famous sons. We'd hear it on the radio —Faubus' Own Fusiliers training in rugged mountainous country. Strom Thurmond's Light Horse is now

on maneuvers. Bull Connor's Canines and Volunteer
Armored Truck being organized. And things like that.
Didn't worry us at all, honey.

"And in the meantime there was daily agitation
in the General Assembly of the United Nations. We
were voted in and vetoed out on the same day. Mister
Eddie, the U.S. Ambassador, he said, 'We cannot
allow these people to non-violent their way into the
U.N.' "

"Oh my."

"It's just like I tell you, honey. And old Lance he
got on our radio station WEBDuBois and he said, My
government has instructed me to say that we will come
in to the U.N. when and if we decide to come in, and
when we *do* we will come in by the front door. Let's
get it straight, Lance says. Says, All we are doing up
here is we are laying a claim on this earth in the great
old American tradition.

"Yes, it was a sad sad time for Lance Huggins,
children. I am alluding to the fact that Miss Brindle,
the love of his heart, was cut off from the soil of Harlem. A daughter of the black bourgeoisie she was living
in Teaneck, New Jersey, practically a prisoner of her
father, a big insurance man in the insurance business."

"That thing of class," Jomo said. "So archaic."

"Bless your soul, honey, it surely was. Well, now,
what was Lance going to do? The whole world knew
where his heart was and all were waiting for him to
play his hand and be the bold black ace. Lance's former wife, the very popular songstress Miss Susan
Brune . . ."

"Odd morality," Shabad murmured.

". . . Miss Brune took to singing a song that caught on like wildfire, called *I'm a broken-hearted bachelor, traveling through this wide world alone.* It became almost her theme song for a while there, and everyone knew to what she was alluding. Miss Susan Brune was a good-hearted woman but she had a touch of the bitterness of an ex. She did not cry; no, not a tear, but there was a melancholy in what she did; and when she sang she let her soul out. She also sang,

Some of those women sure do make me tired,
Gotta handful of gimme, mouthful of much obliged . . .

and subsequent verses embroidered along that general idea, an open attempt to put down poor Miss Brindle of Teaneck.

"Oh yes, honey, it wasn't a very pretty thing, but we had faith in Lance and knew he would not keep us waiting long. In the first days of Harlem we were all filled with daring and do, I assure you of that, and nothing was too much."

"Slick and cunning was the plan," Mboya said.

"Slick *and* cunning was the plan that Lance laid, you are right about that, honey, and in dark of night a commando of twenty picked men, including yours truly—I was temporarily released from duty at Checkpoint Frederick Douglass, which was my post—went to the Black House to await further orders as per instructions.

"We didn't know what was up, but the whole town had the word that something was. I can see the scene in retrospect: that room, and all us men so young, oh my. Well, there we were and ten o'clock went by and then it was eleven. One man said, 'If they don't show by midnight, I'm going to cut out.'

"Stack Purdy, who was later to be my captain and one of the chief architects of the put-down of the invasion, he was there that night, and Stack looked at this man and simply said, 'Do that; and try and write me someday.'

" 'Well, I don't like to just throw away my time,' the other fella says.

" 'And Stack simply said, 'We are all soldiers here,' says.

"And that was the simple truth and the fella knew it. His name was Jim Bowman and he later died, finished his run in a rear guard action on upper Park Avenue, during the time of the Colored Invasion Army. Yes, it's sad, but we all got to pay that debt someday."

The old man fell silent.

Sekou said, "I suppose you must have been pretty tired by then, Grandpa."

"I was beat to my socks," the old man said. "So true, honey, for I had been on duty at my post that whole livelong day; and now here it was, going on midnight. I can't deny it, I did not know how ever in this world I'd make morning on my feet, that I must confess; but I was boyish, don't forget, and hadn't yet learned the lesson of how much strength is in us to be called on.

"I soon found out. Before too much longer, Art Rustram walked in."

"Our first Foreign Minister," Ahmed said.

"Tooby sure he was, honey; and for my particular use, one of the finest and purest young men I have ever met up with in all my days and time. I'll tell you all about him another day if you are good children, for right now he is leading us down the corridor and in to Lance Huggins' own private office, and it was my first sight of Lance close up.

"The whole world knows what he looked like: you've seen the statues, paintings and photographs of his likeness; but I saw him in the glory of his living-ness. He was a real man, let me tell you, and scarred from head to toe with non-violent scars. It would take a man years of really working at it to gather all those scars. Yes, like he used to say, I am a living monument to the fact that the Privileged People have solved every problem but the problem of human relations.

"Too bitterly true, isn't it, honey? But here we are now in Lance's own office and he's shaking our hands and calling us brother. My young heart over-flowed; right then and there I knew I was for him and always would be, and so I was. Lance was a long, clean-shaven, and slender man. Calm, cool, and collected would have described him to a T.

"He walked around behind his desk. It was covered with papers. He picked up a pen and he said, Brothers, says, brothers, tonight's the night and I'm asking you to join me on a personal mission. We're going up the river to bring back Miss Brindle from the

Other Side. Anyone doesn't want to go has only got to say so and no hard feelings.

"He waited and looked around but no one stepped forward or said a word in the negative. Oh I tell you there was no one could beat Lance at getting a Yes out of people; no, not even if their hearts were made of marble stone.

"Lance says, So as to make this strictly legal and not wanting to be accused of taking what is not ours, such as a boat, I am now about to sign the papers nationalising the Hudson River Day Line. You are witnesses, he says.

"Then he signed the papers; he signed them six times in all; looked up at us and smiled and simply said, This is the very same pen I used last week to nationalize every stick and stone of property in Harlem.

"Lance was alluding to the Harlem Land Reform, which was the first act of the new government; and you should have heard the Majority People cry. Oh it hit them where they live and it was sad to see, the way they gave themselves away, no shame at all. All the rents were then cut in half and we paid them to the government. It worked out fine, one of the neatest ideas Lance ever had.

"Lance handed the papers over to José Velasquez, a Puerto Rican gentleman who was the first Minister of Finance we ever had. He came from East Harlem and had formerly been a certified public accountant. There wasn't anything he did not know on the subject of money. Lance says to him, Brother, soon as the bonds are printed, send them in the amount noted to the Hudson Day Line people.

"They'll have to wait twenty-five years, Lance says to us, before they can cash them in. But what else can we do? Everytime we gave the Majority People a dollar they gave us back a lousy dime and now we don't have any ready money. Just don't have it, says.

"Stack looked at his watch, says, 'Lance, brother, it's time to cut out.'

"Lance stood up and buttoned his coat.

"Art Rustram said, 'Lance, you planning on going on this little mission?'

"Oh my, Lance says, here we go again, another lecture on my personal safety, I suppose.

"Art replied, 'It's just a little job and we can pull it off without you.'

"Know you can, Lance simply said.

"Art gave up, and said, 'Well, if you trip this time, you'll trip no more.'

"Lance just shook his head. I wouldn't stop now if I saw myself dying, he said.

"So we went over to the river and 129th Street, to where the Day Line boat was tied up to its pier; went in three cars as black as that night was and pulled up fast, sharp and sudden by the side of the boat, and piled out like hot shots.

"We went on board, and experienced merchant seaman among us got up the steam or whatever; and we set forth on that now famous and historical boat ride when Lance Huggins claimed his own for himself.

"Lance was dressed all in black, a hard-hitting

midnight blue suit and matching coat, which fitted the needs of the occasion and was also proper to the dignity of his position in life. Lance was tense but not nervous. He stood at the furthermost point of the ship, what is called the prow, so great was his eagerness to reach the arms of his loved one by a minute sooner. He looked back once at the shore we had left and these were the words he uttered; said, I go weak in my limbs, brothers, when I think I may never see Harlem again in life."

Little Ngomo began to cry. The old gentleman took the boy on his lap.

"Now don't you worry, honey. Old Lance is going to come out of this scrape for sure. Well then, I will pursue projecting the tale.

"It was a dark dark night. It had been specially picked for that reason, the sky being without a moon at that time of the month. The thing I remember most emphatically about that night was its complete darkness and the moment when Starboard Lookout—a dear friend of mine named Ahearn Tucker who died a natural death a little while back—heard the peculiar and awful sound of the motor of the Coast Guard patrol boat.

"Honey, I have to confess, my heart too struck fear at that particular minute. My left side was jumping. Well, captain cut the engine and we waited in the stillness, we waited in the dark night. We were in the middle of the river, we were at the place called No Return.

"I could see Lance's face. I could see his heart

had struck sorrow at the thought of capture now. There was a price on his head, you know, put there by trifling people who waited impatiently to celebrate his disappearance from this everyday world of ours. I prayed, Lord! Give this good man a break!"

The old gentleman paused to comfort Ngomo.

Jomo said, "It was as if you had all found a home in the rock."

"Well, honey," the old man said, "I will tell you how it seemed to me. It seemed to me we had found a home in the rock, for that mean patrol boat just passed us by, came close to the place where it nearly grazed our sides, and then just went on about its business.

"We proceeded upriver to the George Washington Bridge, where the scene of the rendezvous was scheduled to take place. That run-in with the patrollers had delayed us—it was a setback alright—and Lance was worried. He was jumpy. When Art brought him a sandwich and a cup of hot coffee he turned it aside. I knew just how he felt, for if a sandwich or other food had been presented to me at that time, I was certain my teeth would refuse to bite; and I was hungry from my head down to my feet.

"Well, we slipped right up the middle of the river, coasting along just as smooth as you please, and pretty soon we were in the shadow of the bridge. Captain cut the engine and in the silence he thereby made we could hear their automobiles traveling to and fro on the bridge above our heads. Yes, there they were, enjoying their expensive freedom.

"Captain slowed down and dropped the anchor,"

the old gentleman said. "And now here comes the tricky part of this whole operation."

"Oh my," Ngomo said.

"I was under the bridge, that's where I was; under the bridge and we could see no light or sign of Miss Brindle on the shore.

"Captain puts down his spy glass and he shakes his head. Says to Lance, says, 'Well, Lance,' says, 'what do you think, brother?'

"Only one way to find out for sure, Lance says; and he steps into the lifeboat with yours truly and a lad named Josea Boutwell and Art Rustram, who loved Lance like a son his father, right after him. We lowered away . . ."

"This is the tricky part," Ahmed said.

"Bless your heart, honey, it surely was. It was the tricky part all right for we had no idea what awaited for us on the dark shore, which was double dark as it was further hid by the shadow of the bridge. I will tell you how it seemed to me. It seemed to me that every stroke at those oars taken us into a deeper and deeper darkness and that I would never again see day or the soil of Harlem, our city. Yes, we were steering a straight and swift course and heading right into un-friendly country."

Little Ngomo clasped his grandfather's hand.

"It was just about two o'clock in the morning when the boat scraped up on the land, and let me tell you, children, it was a pleasant sound to these ears for if there is one thing I do not like it is the idea of nothing under me but water. It's not natural. Besides, rivers are sad.

"Lance stepped ashore. It had begun to drizzle. Rain was falling on me. Crystal! Lance whispered. Crystal darling, are you here? Lance said. We did not dare to breathe. Lance was now no where to be seen; he had disappeared in the darkness, which was thick, let me tell you. And on top of that the rain too.

"Crystal, Lance called in a whisper, where are you, dearest? My darling girl, are you here?

"We could hear him from where we were. I was kneeling in the front of the boat where it comes to a point; Josea stood in the back, holding the boat to land with an oar tucked under his arm; Art Rustram was on shore, in the grass up to his knees, the boat's rope wrapped around his hand. He held it taut. Oh my but it was stretched tight! Tight as my nerves at that minute, I don't mind confessing. That was the shape I was in, so worried in heart at the thought of Lance in the darkness, wandering and perhaps lost to us. Every man is subject to a losing day, you know. This project was beginning to take effect on me. My left side was jumping again and my nerves were weakening down, when suddenly there was a little flash of light—'Oh, oh,' I said to myself—that blinked like an eye and went dark just as fast. It was the signal. We did not stir a breath. And soon we heard footsteps.

"Well, I won't keep you waiting, it was Lance and Miss Brindle and, with them, two men, two of our people who lived on the Outside and who had made the arrangements for her get-away. They carried a trunk and any number of suitcases, for Miss Brindle had brought a whole wardrobe with her.

"Crystal," the old gentleman said. "I tell you, she was well named for sure and really something to see. She was so beautiful it was a shame. Oh the way that woman spread her wings! She flew to my head like wine. No wonder Lance had almost thrown himself away for love of her." He fell silent and cupped the warm bowl of the pipe in his bony hands.

Mboya said, "I suppose she was a tall woman."

The old man nodded. "Yes, honey, you are right in your guess. Oh how she glowed! She lit up the darkness like a little old bonfire and was wrapt in furs against the night's damp.

"We loaded the boat with her bundles and trunk and she and Lance took their places on the wide seat at the back of our trusty lifeboat. Art Rustram turned go of the land and we rowed back to the former Hudson Day Liner where silent and jubilant hands raised us up to the deck.

"We skimmed back down the river to the 129th Street pier. That ship knew it was heading for home and wasted not a minute of time. I was in captain's cabin, helping to brew hot coffee that would take the chill from off our bones. Captain first of all poured out two cups, one for Lance and the other for Miss Brindle. It was cozy there in captain's cabin; made me feel like I had friends for miles around.

"Captain took a flacket out of his pocket, it was made of silver, and he poured a drop of spirits in each cup; says, 'The Irish call it Irish coffee. It will take the chill off Lance and warm him and his bride to their heart of hearts.'

"I carried it to them. Yes, it was yours truly who did it. Lance and his beloved were standing arm in arm at the tip of the liner. He was so engrossed in Miss Brindle he hardly knew I was there and just shook his head when I asked would he like something hot. Crystal took a cup and I gave the other to Art Rustram who was standing nearby, keeping watch over Lance, which was his natural custom as well as his duty. It was the first time he had laid eyes on Miss Brindle and his gaze never left her. I don't blame him. He was Lance's nephew, he had all of Lance's trust; and he did what he should not have done—there's no denying it—but I can't blame him, no.

"As I walked away I heard Lance say to Miss Brindle, I heard him say, Dearest, I love to look in your face.

"Well, it wasn't long thereafter that we turned into 129th Street and delivered Miss Brindle safely to Harlem. Yes, she was our first First Lady and I will not be the one to speak harshly of her no matter the sad sad events that later befell, which maybe I will tell you someday."

"I guess that Harlem was mighty jubilant next morning when the news of the wedding broke out," Mboya said.

"You are speaking the truth, honey. And I was mighty happy myself when I stepped off that ship and felt the solid earth of Harlem under my feet. I don't mind telling you I was in a condition of quiet jubilation. Yes, when these two feet touched the old soil it gave my poor heart ease.

"By motor cavalcade we then went, carrying Lance and his beloved to her new and rightful home. They were holding hands like young lovers and it was dawn of one of Harlem's earliest days which is when all this took place, which I have just related, and known as The Day of Miss Brindle."

THREE

"Harlem was two months old and before you could catch your breath it was summer," the old gentleman said. "That's the way it is up here in this north: no spring, nothing in between, no; no intermission of any kind. One day you witness a lot of folks standing around in their heaviest suits saying, 'Oh if I can just make June, July and August'—and the very next day they have got it made.

"Oh now I'm not saying it occurs all the time, but very seldom it doesn't. Once every so often you get a nice day or two that might be called spring if you want to stretch a point. I'm not complaining. Now where was I?"

"Third Avenue and 97th Street," Sekou said, "and it was the first summer of Harlem."

"So right, honey. I am talking about right there at the dividing line, the south frontier, where Luthuli

31

Drive ends and their Third Avenue begins. You been
there. You know it."

"Yes, sir," Sekou said, and he whispered to
Ahmed, "*Il est très désagréable aujourd'hui.*"

"All right now!" the old gentleman said, "that is
really it! Well, that takes the cake! I'm not telling this
tale for my health's sake, you know. I am only telling
it because you begged to hear it—and I consider that
kind of talk way out of line."

The old man waited for absolute silence. "I'd just
as soon go down to the lodge as stay here and tell
stories to bad children."

Sekou began to cry.

"Now don't be mad at me, honey," the old gentleman said to Sekou. "If I was mean I did not intend
to be. Come on up here and sit next to me while I
project this account of a typical Sunday afternoon
during Harlem's first summer.

"I was close witness to history because right
around that time I was permanently relieved of my
duties at Checkpoint Frederick Douglass and assigned
to the Black House Guards. I had the privilege of
being made a corporal and three Sundays out of every
four I was free to do as my heart dictated. Mostly I
went out strolling with your sainted grandmother; and
when she was on duty at the wall I used to go by
myself, when the weather was up to it, to the barrier at
the south frontier.

"Well, there we were in Harlem's first summer.
We were in freedom and justice at last and we hardly
knew what to do with it at first except enjoy it. Which

we did. I tell you, children, there was no end of enthusiasm; it knew no bounds and there was a great
deal of love and affection displayed on those Sunday
afternoons of our first summer when old friends met at
the barrier.

"There were two complete and distinct sets of
barriers, let me set you straight on that. The Majority
People had theirs and we, not desirous of being put
down in any way, set up our own. We had some of
those left behind by the Edison people, which had
hitherto said 'Dig We Must' et cetera. We repainted
them with slogans of our own, famous sayings by our
famous sons, such as, 'The problem of the twentieth
century is the problem of the color line—'

"We also had barriers bearing the famous sayings
that Lance had uttered in the first days of Harlem,
such as, 'We shall be a living petition'—and 'Peace is
the presence of justice'—and 'Not going to let nobody
turn me round.' They were truly beautiful.

"Those Sunday afternoons," the old gentleman
said. "Anybody desirous of taking a stroll knew in
which direction to saunter, for down there at the barriers there were many sights to see, our folks on this
side and the Privileged People on the other. Seems no
longer ago than the week before last."

After a silence Ahmed said, "I suppose there are
some feelings you can't ever lose."

"Too true, honey," the old man said. "It is a fact:
there are some feelings you can't ever lose. My heart
was out for those people, former lovers and friends
now separate, the old Edison barriers between them

and they with tears standing in their eyes. You would have witnessed sights down there that would have cut off your happy days. Just remembering it has torn up my mind—that's why I'm so confused. It's an old sorrow."

"I suppose some of those old friends and lovers brought flowers and other gifts," Jomo said.

"I'm getting to that, honey. Yes, you would often see a member of the Majority People with a large floral offering in her hands which she would throw across the barriers; and she'd say, 'Cora, Cora, tell me it isn't true that you're never coming back to us.'

"And this Cora—one of our people, a large woman, I remember her distinctly—saying, 'Honey, it's really a shame things have to be this way after all our striving.'

"And the Majority Lady says, 'Cora honey, we miss you. Harry says nobody makes potato pancakes like yours. And little Shelly cries every night and refusing to practise his piano.'

" 'Oh my,' Cora says. 'Well, honey, you give that angel child a big kiss for me.'

" 'You eating all right, Cora? You getting enough to eat and all? I read in the papers you people are suffering shortages.'

"Cora says, 'Honey, don't you worry at all; the finest food in the world prevails up here.'

"And there were some very well-dressed Majority Gentlemen who frequented the corner there, striving to see their old friends, even if only a glimpse. They brought gifts, expensive in nature, and strived to reach across the barriers to touch hands with an old friend.

"I remember one in particular. Bluest eyes I have ever seen. He had an old friend on our side, a thin lad named Carl. I used to see the lad around but I haven't seen him for quite a while now. He was one of those boys it was a miracle how they lived.

"The Majority man was so sad it was a shame. He says, 'Carl, I just can't believe it that it should be like this for now and ever after on.'

" 'We had some fine moments,' Carl says.

" 'Is there no chance at all for me?' the Majority Gentleman says. 'Carl, remember how the world used to seem so happy and gay?'

"Carl nodded his head. Oh I tell you my heart went out for him. He looked down at that nicely wrapped little gift in his hand and never did he look up again. 'Friend,' he says, 'do not, I repeat do not, come back up here again,' he says, 'for my poor heart can't stand much more of it.'

"Children, you should have seen the look on that poor Majority Man's face when he realized Carl was saying his last goodbye.

" 'Say it isn't really true, Carl,' this gentleman said, stretching forth his hand. 'Say it isn't really true!'

"But Carl had turned his face away and as he went up Luthuli Drive I heard him say, 'Damn your unhardlucky soul.'

"Yes, honey, there was sadness and bitterness both because we hardly knew what in this world it's best to do. I personally accepted the rightness of our cause, as I do not have to tell you, but there were some other citizens whose minds were all torn up about it. Some said to themselves, 'Lord, this has got to end,' and when it showed no signs of ending they broke up by degrees. Well, they had got used to other ways and one night when it got too much for them they put on their best suit and cut out for down town, old friends, and loved places. You know how it is, some old loves cannot be turned go of.

"Lance made one of his fireside chats in the first days of Harlem, addressing himself to this problem. Brothers, he says, there is no doubt about it: a revolution is an upsetting thing. He says, Some are leaving us, it's true, but others come every day to take their place; these children of ours have been cut every way but loose and we got to be understanding.

"Lance was in fine shape that day and it was one of the most memorable chats he ever made. He said, Those children of ours who are leaving, he says, they must be feeling the worst feelings a man has ever had.

"I don't think there was a dry eye in the house by the time he finished that chat. He hit the nail on the head every time. Back in those first days of Harlem I personally had only a faint idea of what separation meant. The sights I glimpsed at the barrier gave me a glimmer. It was a foretaste. Because when winter came and the cold set in, the crowds broke up by degrees and got smaller and smaller, and by the end of October only a few hardy couples were left. They shivered in their coats and were full of sorrow, knowing the end was near.

"I heard one Majority Man say—oh I tell you, children, it was heart breaking—I heard him say, 'Angel, don't quit me now, dearest, not yet a while.' And she just shaking her head, at a loss for words. 'Since you left me, dearest,' he says, 'I just can't eat a bite, and I have no dreams but bad ones. I can't control my mind, dear, when I think of the future and all.'

"That must have been their last goodbye, theirs and those few other couples too, for nothing could survive a winter like that one was, oh my it was hard. The next Sunday I went down there, just to see. Nobody. Nothing but barriers and border guards, theirs and ours, and no human traffic at all.

"It was then I knew how total we were and that the siege was going to last and last. I stood there a long time, until the weather got a hold of me and I felt stiff in the joints. The cold went spang through me and right to the heart. I put out for home and that was the first time I noticed the absence of white. I had been too busy up to then to see how powerfully lacking it was. It was a jolt, let me tell you. I mean we were in freedom, true, but we were also completely cut loose.

"I walked back to my room as fast as I could go, and I sat on the bed and prayed for someone to knock upon my door."

FOUR

"I want to bring the story on up toward the middle of the first year of Harlem," the old gentleman said. "That means leaving certain things out of account for now and including some others from what was then still in the future." The old man shook his head.

"That's history for you," Jomo said.

"Too true, honey. Every time you try to tell its story it leaves you in a fix. Oh yes, it's hard to keep it straight; for once you begin to line out a history it keeps leading you every whichawhere. It stuns me to think about it. Well, we will just have to stick with it and follow where it leads. I'm not going to let it shipwreck me.

"What I'm going to tell you now are the natural facts touching on Miss Brindle and Art Rustram, which is a sad, sad story.

"This thing about Miss Brindle settled on my

39

brain a long time ago but it still hurts my tongue to talk about it."

"History has been unfair to her," Sekou said.

"Tooby sure it has, honey," the old man said, "and I don't want to make a big fuss over it but that is pure and simply what happened: history has been unfair to Miss Brindle. History has put her way over in the corner, where the shadows are; and she was a woman, when she was still among the living, who was always way out in front. Oh she had something on the ball all right. And beautiful? You can search the whole world over and you will never find her likes. For beauty, style and debonairness Miss Brindle could not be beat.

"Children, you know the story the way the books tell it. All I'm going to do is tell it with heart and a little more sumptuously, for I was a witness and know the circumstances to a T. I'm going to give it to you straight, don't you worry about that. You trust my word, don't you?—All right then.

"Well now, here's how it was from the word Go. I'm trying to take it from the top and follow it right on through. No fooling around now! If you don't want to get jumped on, don't distract me!"

The old man waited for complete silence, lit his pipe, and began:

"Art Rustram was a youngster just coming up along in those times I'm now touching on. He was a lad with a lot of appeal, knew how to dress and handle himself, and had been a famous sportsman in track and field both in his college days.

"He had been born very far south; it was so far south it was somewhere below Zero, Mississippi, just to give you some idea. You can't get down much farther than that. He was no town man. In the beginning, Harlem was like an unknown land to him.

"I can't find praise high enough for Art Rustram, the way he fought for the freedom we needed so bad. While he was still on the Other Side, before Harlem was ever founded—out there in the Kingdom of Bang and Grab, as dear old Lance used to call it—he was in jail as often as he was out. He could sit-in, stand-in, lay-down and stall-in with the best of them. He was like sand in the Majority People's machinery. When it came to a non-violent charge into some governor's personal office, he led the way like a knight of old, noble and debonair from the ground up.

"The mayors of seven different northern cities knew his face; and he once out-pacified a Long Island high school principal, single-handed. And let me tell you, children, that took some doing, it wasn't easy. That lad brandished non-violence like a sword and he was always way out in front where the action was.

"Art was Lance's nephew, his sister's only boy; but in those early days it did not matter who you knew. You had to prove yourself and make your own name. Those pioneer days called out the best in us and we had to show our stuff or else take a back seat. And of all those youngsters coming up in those times Art Rustram was number one; no doubt about it, he was the cat's whiskers, a comer, and his future looked very bright. I mean the lad had everything going for him.

"And then Miss Brindle appeared on the scene. Well, children, please don't go tell your mommas I said so, but the panic was on, it was really on. They tried every whichaway to control it, I believe they did; but it soon began to tear up their minds something terrible. Oh it was sad to see.

"Some say she robbed him of his glory, which he had won with his hardihood; but I say she just couldn't help herself, no more than he could. She fought the thing, I'll swear to that. Miss Brindle fought it body and soul, didn't even know what it was at first. Oh she was a rose and it was sad to see her fading.

"I'd see her sitting in her room, on the little balcony, reclining in an easy chair, all alone. She took to confiding in me; well, I was always around, being a corporal in the Guards, and handy to lend an ear. One day along in those times—I never shall forget that day—we were on the balcony, just the two of us, observing the jubilant scene taking place below.

"I won't keep you waiting another minute. It was the day that Lance opened all the hock shops and said, Come and get it. You would have witnessed a lot of happy faces if you had been making the scene in those far-off times. People of all walks of life could be seen coming from the hock stores, bearing their dear old transistor radios, teevees, and carrying trunks, suitcases, and guitars they hadn't seen for years.

"Lance simply said, We have driven the interest takers out of their temples and now we are abolishing interest itself. All those silent transistors, he says, those long unplucked guitars, suitcases going nowhere, trunks that have known the Greyhound's innards, he says, coats bearing the mark of hock shops' wire hangers in their shoulders, says, all those rightfully belong to you and you shall have them.

"You have paid for them, he says. You have paid for them three times and four times over. They are yours. Come and get them.

"Well, I don't have to tell you that many a heart was made glad by the pronouncement and Miss Brindle and I watched the citizens marching past. You saw cornets and other horns that had not been blown, some of them, for years; but they were all being blown now. What an uproar; I mean it really wailed, and the citizens were jubilant. Oh my.

"And there was Miss Brindle, poor girl, sad amidst the general joy. My heart overwelled just to look at her. Because I knew what it was all about, boyish though I was. God made Miss Eve, I said to myself. I was born Baptist and raised on the Baptist side, as you all know, and being a Baptist just naturally clues you in to a situation such as this one.

"Miss Brindle wasn't swayed by the music, the general joy didn't make dent number one in her sadness. 'Brother,' she said, 'put down your submachinegun, sit beside me, and let me talk myself out to you, for I can see you have an understanding heart.'

"That's what she said, her exact words as I remember them, and I did as she requested. She turned her head and looked out at the Harlem scene, and at the high buildings on the Other Side, and maybe over to New Jersey where her temporary home had been;

and she said to me, she said, 'Sugar, isn't this a mean world to try to live in here.'

"My heart went right out to her. All that music in the streets and the generally jubilant atmosphere dimmed away; it just went, I mean. I could feel it go and I said to myself, Sadness, please don't jump on me. I mean I didn't want any of it. Oh it's hard; I mean it's hard to stand clear when the wreckage is falling all around you.

"She said, 'I'm a stranger here, kin and friends so far away on the Other Side. Lance says they are in the iron cage but I don't know. Sometimes I feel there is nobody to feel and care for me.'

"I tried to ease her mind. 'Honey,' I said, 'everybody loves you. You're the First Lady of Harlem.'

" 'Don't know what it is,' she says. 'Don't know what it is, this burning.' And she put her hand to her heart and simply said, 'This burning burns me.'

"Had I known then the way it was all going to end I would have tried to break it up by degrees. I don't know how in the world I could have done so, but I surely would have tried. Young as I was in those times, just a boy coming up, I knew we were the Righteous People and I knew nothing but trouble and sadness awaited for us in a situation such as this one.

"Miss Brindle she began to cry, and said, 'I'm all torn up inwardly, brother, and I am full of sorrow and I don't even know where it's coming from.'

"Poor girl, she was wood for the burning which had seized her. I mean she was in the clutches of desire. 'Isn't there anything can solace me?' she said.

And she said, 'What can recomfort me for this grievous life?'—I never shall forget her words.

"I had to leave her then to return to my post. Duty called and I was a soldier. And I knew there wasn't a thing I could do for her and I wished there was something to take her off my mind. Yes, Miss Brindle had a lot of suffering laid out for her; and so did Art. He had the poor man's heart disease. He already had the look on his face, that look which says, You've made me throw my only friend down. And that's one of the worst feelings a man can ever have."

"I guess a shameful ending was in store for them," Sekou said, breaking the silence.

"It is your bedtime now, honey; and besides, it's a long and sad sad story and I don't feel like telling the rest of it now. If you ever been down, then you know just how I feel. I mean really down."

FIVE

The old gentleman said, "We were in hard luck when the time came for Harlem's first Christmas.—You sure I haven't told you this story more or less recently?"

"No, sir!" Jomo said.

"All right then. Well, in that case, honey, I will proceed to tell it. Well, we were in hard luck when the time came for Harlem's first Christmas. We had to live in such a way that it was not exactly a pleasure. We had put to the plow all our Central Park lands, from 97th Street to Harlem Meer. I used to go on my Sundays off and lend a hand out of old experience, the longing to do, and the wanting to volunteer. You would have been astonished to witness the numbers of people out there who had never seen the under side of a clod of earth before.

"So, we had a crop in the ground alright but it was hard luck or maybe that ground wasn't used to it. Seeds and the hoe upset it after all those years during

47

which time it had fed on nothing more substantial than soot. Then too it had been one of those no rain summers, what we used to call down home a drought. Oh it was a dry season, let me tell you. We carried water by the bucket from Harlem Meer; my hand hasn't forgot it yet.

"And on top of that, on top of that, honey, it was a *swift* summer. Cut out and said goodbye before your back was turned. That's the way it goes, children; you may get a pardon and you may drop dead, as we used to say. Before I knew what happened, snow was falling down on me. And I had no coat to suit the weather!

"But it was in my boyish days, honey, don't forget, and I could stand to catch a lot of hell—don't tell your mommas—in those bygone times.

"Well, children, now here is how it was: it wasn't just the cold, so sudden and soon as it was and hard as salt, no; it was firstly the question of food supplies. They were low. My but they were low. The fact of the matter is, we were at the place where it was famine."

"Oh, oh."

"And Lance and the government was still where the national treasury was just beginning to build up, and we were thusly in a state of temporary financial embarrassment. It was terrible. We were in an awful fix.

"The only funds we had at that time came from the checkpoints and the rents—it was before we nationalised the numbers. At the checkpoints we laid a toll of ten dollars on every subway train passing through 125th Street. Also the New York Central and the New Haven Railroad lines. Which passed it on to the commuter in the form of higher fares.

"And that was why my first job at Checkpoint Frederick Douglass, before I was promoted to the Guards, was a position of such high responsibility. It was just that, let me tell you. Thousands and thousands of people going to and fro work and they had to go *under* or *over* Harlem to get there. I had the shift which coincided with the rush hours, morning and afternoon, down there in the subway, a place where I had never been before. There was no way round for the Majority People. We had them in our pocket.

"Oh they tried all kinds of countermeasures, not least including the measure of trying to cut off our electricity. It was a dirty shame. There were some very dark nights up here, I want you to know; and a few citizens got a little jumpy and you would have heard some people saying, 'I wish they'd quit it so far as this turning off the lights goes.' They were dismayed. 'Makes me feel I'm on my last go-round,' man said to me. I personally was fresh from the country and lights out was no big deal for me. Catch me making a fuss over something trivial of that nature. Some people acted like it was shortening down their days. But it didn't last only a short while.

"We held the big ace, the bold card, and we played it, we slapped it down right on the line by putting a stop to all trains going through by means of obstructions on the tracks. In no time at all the Privileged People turned on the lights and it was because we had brought them to a standstill.

"That was the way it went. We kept the Majority People worried all the time. Measure and counter-measure, as Lance said. Said, Fear not, brothers and sisters. They are giving us a hard way to go, that's true; they are trying to shipwreck us and we are in a bad condition, that's true; old bad luck seems to follow us each and everywhere, that's true; *but,* when one door closes, another opens.

"And once again Lance was proved right," the old gentleman said, and he fell silent.

"Rationing was declared as a first step, I guess," Mboya said.

"You know your onions, honey. Rationing *was* declared as a first step and the citizens took it in stride and took it orderly. We would all get in line at one or the other of the Great African & Pan-Islamic cooperative grocery chain, and it soon became a place where you could always count on companionship and good talk, which is a thing I crave.

"I never shall forget those days of standing in line with my little green card stamped *Bachelor, No Kith or Kin, Member of Armed Forces,* and stamped with Lance's beautiful signature. Oh he had a very pretty hand among other things. I have certainly got that card somewhere in my trunk."

"I suppose you got into a lot of conversations while waiting on the line, Grandfather," Sekou said.

"I was about to tell you about that, honey," the old man said, and he slowly drew his pipe back to life before continuing. "So there I was on the line one day—it was the day before Christmas which is why I remember it so emphatically—waiting to receive the ration of bacon and bread being dispensed that special day, and this little old lady wearing glasses standing in front of me on the line. She looked like a sensible woman.

"She turned around all the way. She looked at me, and she said, 'You appear to be a nice boy and I will tell you something that is troubling me to my very soul.'

" 'Why surely I'll be glad to listen, sister,' I says to her.

" 'Well,' she says, 'this morning as I was coming down the stairs,' she says, 'I bunked into an elderly Spanish gentleman who addressed me in his native language.'

" 'Un-hunh,' I says, nodding my head.

" 'He spoke no English at-*all.*'

" 'Un-hunh,' I says.

" 'And I have been worried sick all day as to what he was trying to tell me.'

"For you see, children," the old man whispered, "this was back in the days when only an advanced few like Lance Huggins spoke all the necessary languages."

"Oh, oh," Diego said.

"Bless your heart, honey, but that stage did not last long and in isolation we became what they call multi-national, that was getting the best of all things,

African, Puerto Rican, Chinese, and Gypsy too, as you know.

"So, this lady said to me, 'What do you think that Spanish gentleman was trying to tell me?'

"I told her I did not know, and she simply said, 'Well, it's got me worried. It might have been something important.'

"Yes, honey, it was sad, but that's how it was during the famine. Some people got disheartened and disgusted. 'This famine is taking effect on me,' you'd hear some people say. Or even, 'I may be rolling but it won't be here. You will call me and I'll be gone. I've laid around this town too long. I'm tired of fattening frogs for snakes. Harlem, I'm through with you and I hope you don't feel hurt.'

"Well, honey, it's hard to walk in that straight and narrow way. It's no easy street, you know. But you also heard others say, 'I'm not leaving this hard luck town as long as my blood runs warm. Here I am and I'm feeling very well.'

"And some people got to feeling a little funny; we all seemed to be awaiting for a sign or message to indicate we were not alone, that succor was coming, help at hand, the opening of that door of which Lance spoke.

"There were some people who were at the place where they didn't even care, but that wasn't true of the most of us. One thing I'd like to get across is that spirits were high and people went on in a way that was full of enthusiasm.

"You'd hear a man say, 'Well, it's a bad wind

that never changes,' and there were other encouraging
words that could be heard all over the place, one man
striving to cheer another. You would hear, 'Hard
times don't worry me—I was broke when it first
started out.' Or, 'I'm in a bad condition but I'm going
down *slow.*' And a very popular expression in those
days was, 'Well, brother, I am only halfway worried.'

"Well, that night when I got off duty it came to
me that it was Christmas Eve and all I had waiting for
me in the way of supper was some bread and tea."

"Oh my."

"It seemed like there was no end to the tea we
had, a gift from our Chinese brothers who got it to
Harlem some ways, don't ask me how because I do not
know, although there was a lot of activity down at the
129th Street pier around that time. Lance announced
it on the radio, saying, This is the Boston Tea Party in
reverse, brothers and sisters. And if this be treason,
make the most of it, he says and he brought the house
down. Oh my yes, he had the whole town talking.

"Lance said, That tea cast on the waters those
centuries ago has now returned to us *multiplied!* Well,
children, I don't have to tell you, it was a big day for
the Buddhists. They got out their dragons and lanterns
and made a very colorful parade the length of 125th
Street to the cheers of all."

The old gentleman paused, as if recalling to mind
the sight of the gay festivities.

"It was the first Chrismtas of Harlem," Jomo
said, "and there you are, just getting off duty at the
Black House."

"You are a crackerjack, honey. And didn't I tell you I did not have bite number one waiting for me? —All right then; well, I was in no great hurry to get where I was going so I walked for the warmth and because I did not appreciate returning to an empty room. Remember that it was Christmas Eve and I was a boy far from home and Mother, who was a woman sure to me. I had answered the freedom call and traveled a long way as a result. I had heard the call and before I knew what had hit me, I was sweet Harlem bound. And even in famine's darkest days I did not think my work in vain. I wasn't like those who walked around and laid around saying, 'I don't feel welcome, mama, in Harlem anymore.' It's true we were all catching a lot of hell but don't think I was disheartened, because I wasn't.

"Now, children, don't think hard of me; I tried to be in reason but, children, there was a feeling seemed to tell me that actions and activities, unusual in nature, were afoot that night of Christmas Eve. Didn't know what it was but had the feeling I was walking up to something really big."

"Superstition!" Kenyatta said, sadly. "How strong it must have been!"

"Yes," Sekou said, "two steps forward and one step back, as the Man said."

"You boys want me to pursue this or do you *not* want me to?" the old gentleman said. "I'm not begging.

"I will now continue the tale therefore," the old man said. He cleared his throat, and began: "We were all like that in the famine time. When I was in my room I waited for a knock on the door. When I went to bed I prayed to dream of a mule in my hat. And in the street you would see people looking at each other's faces, hoping for the Word. Some were even so disheartened, really down in the mouth, that they declared it was Harlem's last days."

"*Agents provacateurs,* surely," Sekou said.

"Just badly disheartened citizens, honey. I tell you it was the kind of feeling that leads you don't know where. I felt aimless and lonely, even though by this time I had friends for miles around.

"Well, there I am, coming out of the Black House; and I walked without goal, and before I knew it I was at the city's south frontier, where Franklin Frazier Avenue ends and Lexington begins. Our militia people had little fires going in iron barrels to keep warm by. They had their backs to the wind and their hands outstretched to the warmth. Members of the ladies auxiliary soon arrived on the scene to dispense mugs of hot tea. I looked around for your grandmother and after a little while I spotted her; she was there and pretty as a girl can be, with her rifle in her hands.

"I hung around to listen to our militia people sing. For the least significant occasion we would always have some music, you know. They gave a special feeling to the lines: *He made me a watchman upon a city wall.* It was a wonder to the ears. That very pretty hymn was number one in the militia song book; it was their masterpiece. Oh it was joyful to hear and I remarked on the fact that the Federals facing us, those poor souls, turned off their transistors to listen.

"I had a cup of tea and having joined in the good conversation there, was surprised beyond words when who did I run up with?—That same nice old lady who had addressed me on the ration line. She was asking around for the elderly Spanish gentleman. She says to me, says, 'Son, don't I know you from somewhere?'

"Poor soul did not know which way to turn next, I guess. Militia people gave her a cup of tea and listened to her story. They kindly reassured the lady that should they catch sight of the gentleman in question, they would find out what he had to say, for there were many Spanish speaking soldiers among them, including the famous volunteers from the Lower East Side, members of the famous Campos Brigade who infiltrated Washington Heights during the War of Nerves period.

"She thanked them and for the tea also. She said, 'Thank you, boys, from the bottom of this tired old heart.' She says, 'I will continue keeping my own eyes peeled and if I find the gentleman, why, I'll bring him to you boys for translation; for a feeling tells me that he has something important to say.'

"She went off on her own way, she went away happy because she had someone to tell her troubles to; but I don't mind telling you she left a troubled silence behind her.

"Well, I stayed with your grandmother till the tea break was over, my boyish eyes enjoying the sight of rifles stacked in the prescribed way and the smartness of our military men. Those rifles never had better care, let me tell you, I don't care where they came from; in the light of the fires they sparkled like all get out. And when it came to smartness, our militia just could not be beat. But mainly there was a companionship that pacified my mind, and when I left them I no longer felt shipwrecked. A feeling told me that we were already approaching the far shore, safety at hand.

"Yes, walking back uptown I could feel words of joy preparing themselves in my mouth. That is why I was not one bit surprised to see the crowd gathered, I think it was at 121st Street. It was clear to me that a parade was shaping up and I wondered what it was all about. Some of the men were carrying those torches where the fire drips off them like wax. Oh it was a pretty sight, the procession moving off, up Lenox, and I ran after and hooked on to the end of the line. I applied directly to the gentleman on my right and I said to him, I said, 'What is this all about if you wouldn't mind telling me?'

"And this gentleman says to me, 'Lad, you may not believe this, but I don't actually know what this is all about. I happened to be passing by and having nothing else to do I joined in.'

" 'Un-hunh,' I says.

"The gentleman says, 'Where parades are concerned, lad, I have had a long standing weakness. So here I am.'

"And there *I* was, still in the dark. Oh my, it was something. And I began to feel troubled, for what was I doing there not knowing what it was all about, and

me a member of the Black House Guards? For all I
knew those people could have been what Lance called
Divisionists!

"But at that moment the people at the head of the
line struck up a song and put all my doubts to flight.
They were singing:

Oh, Mary what you gonna name
That pretty little baby?

Well, then I knew right off where I was and joined in,
for I had the words right there in my mouth, all ready
to go. They were nice people and I figured them to be
on the way to church for the midnight service.

"We walked quite a way and sang all the while,
arriving finally at 136th Street."

"Harlem Hospital," Jomo said.

"Tooby sure it was, honey. That's exactly the
place we had come to and imagine my astonishment to
see people gathered there by the hundreds, standing
around singly and in groups. I was stunned. When my
contingent joined the throng they were in the middle
of singing, *Wasn't that a mighty day when Jesus Christ*
was born. I recommend that song to all of you for
sheer prettiness.

"I then started milling around, asking this person
and that what was going on. All replied the same. 'Just
waiting to see,' they all said. A lady told me, she said,
'We got a representative inside and I have no doubt
there will be an announcement shortly.'

"So I waited with the rest of them and my but it
was cold. People stamping their feet, and their breaths

were all smoky in the air, you know what that's like. Little fires for warmth sprang up here and there amid the crowd, which soon numbered in the thousands.

"There was no impatience and you did not hear a strident voice. People planted themselves and settled in, and a feeling got to be very strong among us. Not a word was uttered but I believe we all had the same thought: God listens to this world. And we were hopeful of His aid and figured He would send it in the customary way. It was the right time for it; and I still have the feeling that if He was ever going to, He should have made his move then. That was the time to play the Big Ace."

The old man sighed, then continued his tale: "Some of the greatest first-class singing I have ever heard in my lifetime I heard that night. We sang *Rise up, Shepherd, and follow. There's a star in the east on Christmas morn. Rise up, Shepherd, and follow! It'll lead to the place where the Savior's born.*

"As well as other songs similar in nature such as *The Virgin Mary Had a Baby Boy,* without any doubt a really perfect number.

"Oh we did sing that night! We sang till dawn when the rumors began and we went right on with singing until not a single star was left in the sky. I tell you it was a very peculiar night, a mixture of hope combined with a foreboding. Every once in a while the most awful silence would fall on us all. There were many places before dawn where I thought we had come to the end. But no, a voice would begin with

Wasn't that a mighty day or another number, and hope would rise once more in our hearts.

"Peculiar? Well, that wasn't the half of it as you'll agree when I tell you. Not a single baby was born that night at Harlem Hospital! Or at least so we were told by the man inside. He came out in the first light, just stood there and shook his head. Crowd broke up by degrees. There were many among us who took it for a sign, but did not know yet what the sign signified. You would have seen any number of crest-fallen faces at that moment, let me tell you. Hope went down the river; it cut out, it really did.

"And so did yours truly. I walked back down Lenox. I was beat, I don't mind telling you; I was almost dead. And on the way home I fell in with the man I had met previously, the gentleman who loved parades. We strolled side by side for a short while and finally I asked him what line of work was he in, just to get the ball rolling, you know.

" 'I was formerly a census taker,' he says.

" 'Do tell,' I says. 'Was that a good job?'

"And he replied, 'To tell you the honest truth, lad, it was kind of seasonal in nature. But I did get to meet a lot of people.'

" 'Yes,' I says, 'un-hunh, and where was it you engaged in census-taking?'

" 'Right here,' he says, 'right here in dear old Harlem.'

"Well, that came as a surprise to me and that is why it has stuck with me; for hitherto I had not known that we were even among the counted, and I told my companion as much.

"And he said, 'Yes, lad, things have changed up considerable. Formerly we were among the counted, but now we are among the heard.'

"I judged by his way of talking that here was a man who knew his Bible backwards and forewards. I asked him what his church was and he simply replied, 'I personally am eighty per cent Muslim.'

" 'Eighty per cent Muslim,' I says. 'And what does that signify?'

" 'That means I don't want to be white,' he answered.

"Children, please remember how long ago this time was to which I am now alluding. I mean, this was way back. It takes a long time to get rid of old feelings, and there are some you just can't turn go of; you were never stuck with them so you can't judge of it. Take it from me. Old man Noah knows. Now where was I?"

"You were walking home to Black House and it was now Christmas Day," Shabad said.

"That was it, honey. There I was. I was strolling down the avenue, I was in my prime but feeling low, like I had lost everything I ever had and all my friends had turned me down. In the coming months I would get to know that feeling like a book. I recall very distinctly—and you will soon see the reason why—that I stopped in at Miss Susan Brune's bar and grill and ate a soy bean sandwich and a nickel of beer.

"Miss Brune herself came up to me and in her

very famous voice said, 'Corporal, how things, sugar? How's old Lance and the new Missus?'

" 'Just fine, Miss Brune, thank you,' I replied.

"Miss Brune says, 'Honey, I hear our First Missus has eyes for another.'

"When I heard that—you can imagine, children; try to put yourselves in my place and judge of it yourselves—when I heard Miss Brune's words it made my blood run cold. I put down my beer and I said, 'Who told you so? Whoever told you that is a liar, and that's straight from the horse's mouth,' I says. 'You trust my word, don't you?'

"I tell you, children, this once glad heart of mine was really thumping as I said it. I went on, I pursued the subject. 'Miss Brune,' I says, 'it really makes me wild to learn that stories such as this are going the rounds.'

" 'Well, corporal, you know how people talk,' she says.

" 'Whoever told you that story has been paid off,' I says, 'and is playing bad.'

" 'Oh my,' Miss Brune says, 'you do have a faceful of frowns. I'm sorry I ever opened my big mouth; but it has been worrying my mind, for scandal can do our cause no good, no good at all,' she says. She was a true patriot, although due to overagedness—she was somewhere in her thirties—not a member of the militia, and I was sorry I had been sassy to her. She was wearing a dress must have cost over a dollar a yard.

"When I left Miss Brune's I was feeling cold and chill. What she had said didn't do me any good, believe it. My heart overwelled with troubles and with the thought of the hard trials ahead. I did not want any of it; all I wanted was a little wife and a table spread. Some people don't mind marrying but they hate settling down; I personally liked both parts of it. Now where was I?"

"Leaving Miss Brune's and feeling bad."

"You can say that again, honey. I was really down and I stayed that way until later in the day when Lance came on on the radio with his regular Christmas Day Fireside Chat. It was one of his institutions. He took for his text the words: Only Man is brother to Man."

"A pregnant statement," Nkrumah said.

"It really was, honey. Some people had the feeling that Lance had left them high and dry, but they were only a handful. The rest of us now knew what it was all about, which we had not known before.

'Just one more thing I'd finally like to say for it is soon your bedtime, and that is this. The next day was Sunday, children, and what a sad old Sunday that was. It was memorable. You can't imagine."

"I guess that you were all really up against it," Mboya said, but the old man seemed not to hear.

After a little while, Shabad said, "Grandfather, I wonder what that elderly Spanish gentleman wanted to tell the old lady?"

"Bless your soul, honey," the old man said. "That question's been bugging me for a very long time too."

SIX

That was one tough winter," the old man said, filling his pipe. "It really was. Words fail me to describe how it came on."

"Harlem's first winter," Diego said.

"Yes, and I hope you children never see its like," the old gentleman said. "That was the time when the world was really rough. And it was freakish, the goings on and the curious events I am about to allude to."

Little Ngomo edged closer to his grandfather's chair; the old man laid his hand on the boy's head.

"They cut off our fuel and it was so cold in the houses it was a shame. So much thought was given to just keeping warm that it was hard to keep our minds set on freedom. That was the danger and Lance knew it. He always knew, knew each and everything. If there was a prevalence of bad dreams, he knew it. If citizens were sitting in their rooms too much again, he felt it. His finger was on the public's pulse every minute of the day and night. It is great to have ability from extreme to extreme and Lance had it in abundance. Just show me the doubter and I'll show *him*. I'll run him in. And if I can't run him in, I will surely talk him down."

He looked around the room for challengers; there were none and he went on with his tale.

"As I have told you—didn't I tell you?—yes, well, I was close witness to history because around two months after Harlem was founded I was assigned to the Black House. Art Rustram and the others around Lance had prevailed on him to avail himself of something like a bodyguard. At first, Lance would not hear of it. He rebuked them. He took it as an injury to himself. You have got to give yourself to danger, he always said.

"But his staff and the various ministers of government were unusually worried for Lance's safety. This was on account of certain nocturnal activities being perpetrated at that time. Well, it was understandable. Everybody's nerves were weakening down around this time I am now touching on, and the others figured they'd be doing Harlem a real good deal by giving extra protection to Lance's person.

"I don't have to tell you children what a valuable man he was and how we valued him. He was loving, good, and kind. It is all there in your history books and I'm just filling in with some personal memories." The old man paused to light his pipe.

Sekou said, "I guess this must have been around the time of the Colored Invasion Army?"

"Don't push me, boy, or I'll get all the facts confused. We'll get to that and don't you worry, but now here's the thing: Harlem in that first winter was really no place for the comfort-loving to be. The good-timers and the high-livers were disheartened and disgusted —Mr. Livingood and Uncle Yesterday they left on their own will right away—and their feelings were taking effect on a lot of people.

"Well, honey, it's just like I said. There was the shortness of food, there was the complete and total lack of heat, and the only thing we had an abundance of was cold, snow, and those icy winds from the river which were really memorable for coldness. It was terrible.

"Freedom was what we craved and what we then had for the first time here in this dear old city. I mean there wasn't a single Mason-Dixon line in the whole place. And we knew that just across the border in the land of the Privileged there was never enough freedom to go around, although you would not have known it if you had ever lent an ear to Radio Free Harlem. That was the special radio station the Majority People had and used for broadcasting direct to us. It was run by Mister Arthur, a Privileged Person with a famous voice. They would broadcast messages to us from our captive brothers on the Other Side.

"There was one lady of our race we called her Washington, D.C., Rose. She broadcast to us every night at seven, right on the dot, and did us the great big favor of playing our own music back to us, and told all about the joys of her outside freedom—how she could buy all the shoes and all the clothes she wanted.

"She was just throwing away her time. Lance said he hoped we would soon be able to unration such things as shoes and clothes because then, he said, the Privileged People would have to get down to where the heart of the argument really was."

"A famous utterance," Diego said.

"Tooby sure it was, honey, and I never shall forget the day it was uttered and Lance sitting there at the long table, microphone in front of him bearing the letters WEBDuBois, one hand always fiddling around with the shaft of the mike while he talked. It was one of his famous habits and came to be widely imitated by others and needless to say lesser men. Now where was I?"

"Nocturnal activities of a peculiar nature," Sekou said.

"Honey, I'm not up to that part yet. Please don't try to lead this old man astray, boy."

"Lance was making a famous chat on the radio," Ahmed said.

"You have really hit it on the nail that time, honey, that's just where I was up to. Now how did I know I wasn't up to the nocturnal activities?—I'll tell you how I knew: because those peculiar activities did not begin until after the Majority People had tried to buy Lance off!

"That was a sad sad scene when Mister Eddie,

the Majority People's ambassador to the U.N., came up here in his Cadillac, bearing a fat bribe in his hand.

"Now here is the thing: they sent Lance the word by means of diplomatic courier, who was just a young fella in a plain grey suit and he did not pay too much attention to his attire or his place in life. He was passed through at the 97th Street border, down there at Checkpoint George Padmore, I think it was, and escorted to the Black House where he was received with all correct courtesy by a lower ranking member of Lance's staff. It was Jim Hardison who received him and took the envelope from his hand, for that diplomatic courier was jumpy in every limb. He was worried, really worried. Jim said to him—Jim died a natural death not too many years ago—Jim says to him, 'Boy, *re*lax; we are all civilized up here.'

"And there was yours truly, right there in dear old Lance's personal office when Jim comes in with the note. History was forever being made right before my very eyes, let me tell you. It really was something.

"Lance says, Read it to me right away, Jim, for I have the feeling this is what we need and just what the doctor ordered. An event, Lance says, to take our people's minds off the hard times and back on to the subject of freedom, says, where they properly belong.

"Jim read the note; yes, he read it all. Including the rigamarole at the beginning, even though Lance's fingers were drumming away on the desk top, so eager he was to get to the nut.

"My government is seized with the idea and is taken with the notion and according to the letter and the spirit of this and that and the other and paragraph this and sub-paragraph that and so on. Jim read it all, he really did. Well, you couldn't hardly stop him when he once got going. Only a hard-hearted man would have tried. Jim loved it so. And Lance just waited him out, sitting there at his desk as slim and elegant as you please.

"Well, finally Jim gets to the nut. Mister Eddie, their man at the U.N., requests a meeting with Lance to discuss a certain problem. A certain problem. That's what he said and we all had a good laugh over it.

"Whatever can that certain problem be? Lance says. And he says to Jim, Jim, he says, you love the language so, I'm going to ask you to compose a reply. Tell Ambassador Eddie, he says, tell him to come on up here tomorrow afternoon at three on the dot, Eastern Colored Standard Time, and no futzing around, Lance says.

"Jim says, 'Mr. Prime Minister, I shall begin my note as follows: My Government have requested me to say . . .'

"Lance interrupts him right then and there. He says, Jim, says, Jim, where did that *have* crop up from?

"Jim says, 'Lance baby, that is the language of diplomacy and protocol. It really wails.'

"Lance says, Jim, where did you learn all that? You didn't learn it in your former life as a civil service post office clerk.

" 'No,' Jim says, 'no, I did not and that's for sure,

but I have lately been reading up on it in a handbook lent to me by a Nigerian friend with many years of strenuous experience at the U.N.'

"Yes, Lance says, those old nations do know a thing or two. Dear old Nigeria, he says.

"So Jim wrote the reply. It must have been well over one page long and it was really a professional job in every way. We were duly impressed, and Jim felt set up for days. Jim died a natural death not too many years ago. The note was then signed by Art Rustram who was at that time Foreign Minister, which made it his business to deal with foreign countries, so Mister Eddie was thereby right up his alley. That's how these things work, children.

"Well, I won't keep you hanging and I'm not going to bother you with my own personal thoughts at the time, no. Oh they were rough thoughts, let me tell you, and it was on account of that hard hard winter. I pictured Mister Eddie walking up the steps with that little suitcase they all carry, and I thought: Oh oh, bad luck is waiting there too. In those days I saw it waiting everywhere."

"Oh my."

"Yes, honey, the world was really tough at that period. And I thought: All gamblers get broke sometime."

"So true," Sekou said. "And I guess Mister Eddie thought he really had a sly and cunning plan there."

"Tooby sure he did, honey. He thought he really had it made and it was because he didn't know Lance. In my estimation he thought he was still dealing with the old so-called type leaders. You never knew any of those, children, because after Lance we threw away the mold.

"We all felt that way. Dear old Josea Boutwell, still at that time Minister of Interior, I heard him say —we were all standing around the lobby of Black House waiting for Mister Eddie—I heard him say, 'I'll give anybody ten to one he's coming up here with the names of a three-man committee to keep the dear old lines of communications open.'

"There were no takers and as a matter of fact my good friend Ahearn Tucker, who was present in his capacity of Minister of Marine Affairs and Fisheries, says, 'Yes, brother, and whatsmore I can tell you who those committeemen will be: one retired businessman, one retired football coach, and a college professor with a bow tie.'

"Well, there was laughter all around and the various Ministers strived to put on straight faces in preparation for Mister Eddie's appearance. You can all judge that in my position as a member of the Black House Guard I was in the perfect place to get a close up look at things; I mean I was at the place where I could rub shoulders with history.

"Mister Eddie arrived on the dot; I checked my Elgin and he was on the nose. Mister Eddie was a neat dresser but he did not have much hair at all; he also had freckles, now that I think about it."

Jomo said, "Poor souls, they are so susceptible to those scarifying blemishes."

"You said a mouthful there, honey. Well, in he

walked with his little suitcase and a little smile and his
sly and cunning plan. Jim Hardison introduced him
around, enjoying it to the hilt with his Mr. Ambassador this and his Mr. Minister that and so forth and on,
and finally he says, 'Mr. Ambassador,' says, 'since I
know the way, I'll just take the liberty of leading you
to the Prime Minister's office if you don't mind. Just
follow me, sir,' he says.

"In my estimation there was a little strain on both
sides for Mister Eddie's smile had got a little shaky by
now and he was in a condition where the smallest
thing would have made him jump. Well, I strolled
along behind Jim and the Ambassador, playing it cool
as we security men are taught to do, not letting on we
are really there for purposes of protection. Mister
Eddie making polite chatter all the way, saying to Jim
Hardison, you know, like 'Nice place you got here,'
and all.

"Jim says, 'Thank you, Mr. Ambassador, it just
about suits our needs for the present, sir, although we
are thinking about spreading our wings sooner or
later.'

" 'Un hunh,' Mister Eddie says.

"Jim leads him into Lance's personal office.
Lance is wearing a really sweet all black suit and he
says to Mister Eddie, Welcome to Harlem, Ambassador, he says. First time you've been up here, I believe,
he says.

"Mister Eddie says, 'Real pleasure to be here,
Mr. Huggins,' says. Not calling him Mr. Prime Minister, you see, because he was not desirous of indicating

that we had a government of our own. According to the Majority People we weren't even on the map, and any map whatsoever which included us had made a big mistake. We had no recognition whatever in that quarter. Old Jim Hardison, he used to say, 'If I am not *de jure* and if I'm not *de facto,* then what the *hell* am I doing here!'—Now don't tell your mommas I said so.

" 'Uncommon cold winter we're having,' Mister Eddie says, just to get the ball rolling, you know.

"Yes, it surely is and all, Lance says.

" 'Days getting shorter all the time and can't remember the last time I saw sunshine,' Mister Eddie continues.

"Yes, Lance says, sunshine is a very scarce item this winter up here in Harlem. How's the weather in the U.S.A.?

"Mister Eddie says, 'One hears you got a lot of scarce items up here right now.'

"Lance smiled his famous smile and he said to Mister Eddie, Mister Eddie, he says, I am relieved to hear you say that for I was getting to have the feeling that you made the long rough journey up here just to talk about the shape the weather is in. Have a cigar, Mister Eddie, Lance says; and he opens this big box of Havanas he has on his desk.

" 'Why, thank you kindly, sir,' Mister Eddie says, taking one, 'don't mind if I do,' says. 'I haven't seen a real Havana for lo these many years now,' he says.

"So I hear, Lance says. And he says, Take another one for later because we surely do have an ample supply.

"Well, children, you can see how it went and how Mister Eddie came on. Lance showed him up every which way imaginable, and then some. I tell you there was nothing and no one could overlord Lance's true greatness.

"They lit up their cigars and the Majority Man sat back in his chair. He was fully relaxed; but he kept his coat on because he wasn't used to the cold indoors. He must have had the feeling it was still the old days, for that was the feeling he exuded. I felt it; yes, I felt it and for a minute there I don't mind telling you I was dismayed.

"But then I looked at Lance, took just one look and knew the old days had cut out for good and all and were gone, I mean they were really gone; for Lance Huggins' many talents did not include that of sellout artist, no, never. I had no doubts. Dismay turned go of me and I rebuked myself for falling back into old habits of thinking. To change your ways isn't easy, children, and you can ask anybody who has tried. It's really rough.

"Mister Eddie puffed at his cigar. 'Oh my but that is a good smoke,' he says. 'Yes, you have to hand it to those people when it comes to cigars,' he says; and he utters a big sad sigh and declares, 'It really is too bad that your people are having such a rough sad time of it up here.'

"Well, says Lance, if we're having a bad time now, we were given a really rockbottom thorough training for it these past three hundred years and more.

" 'Past is past,' Mister Eddie says and he said it real easy.

"Except when it's present, Lance says.

"Mister Eddie says, 'Yes now, well, as I was saying, it surely is a sad sad thing to see people suffering like this when it's not an absolute necessity.'

"Un-hunh, Lance says, tooby sure it is, but despair is the beginning of wisdom and, you know, Mr. Ambassador, we are not exactly blockading our *selves!* he says. Everything we have has got to be smuggled in here under the noses of your patrollers.

"Mister Eddie says, 'My government have made its policy very very clear. For humanitarian reasons, which are one of our biggest traditions, we are permitting you to import all the groceries and medical supplies you need. The whole world knows that.'

"Uh-hunh, Lance said; and that was all he said, but it was enough to make Mister Eddie cough, for he knew we did not have a dime and could not buy pork chop number one. Mister Eddie was famous for his coughing, children. Down at the U.N. they had a special translator just for his coughs. He was something. 'Like I said,' says Mister Eddie, 'this very sad and unfortunate situation can be alleviated in just a matter of minutes.'

"That so? says Lance and he simply added, I really am glad to hear that, I truly am.

" 'Yes,' the Man says, 'I can give you the solution in a single word.'

"Lance didn't blink; he was really cool and he

simply said, What could that single word be, Mr. Ambassador?

" 'I'll give you the word, Mr. Huggins,' he says. 'I'll give you the word and the word is—*Resign!*'

"Well, I leave it to your own estimation, children, the feelings I felt at that moment and the shape I was in. My left side was jumping and I thought the ground was going to turn go of me. I was in a mist for a while there, I don't mind telling you. Oh it was difficult. But I took hold and said to myself, Watch out now! That's what I said.

"Meantime, Mister Eddie was going on; I mean between coughs he could really go. Says, 'We know, Mr. Huggins, that without you this so-called nation of Harlem will weaken down pretty quick and break up by degrees. And just in case you may be a bit worried about it, my government have asked me to assure you that there will be a complete and total amnesty and no legal recriminations of any kind against anyone is foreseen, at the present time. You people been in a state of rebellion against the legally recognized government, and you haven't been paying any rent at all, but we are just going to forget it. Bygones are one of our biggest traditions, as the whole world knows; and past is past, like I said.'

"Lance nodded his head every once in so often, letting the Man know he was taking it all in. Un-hunh, he says every now and then, out of politeness, you know. Then Mister Eddie says, 'I don't need to tell you, Mr. Huggins, how very very grateful my government are prepared to be for your cooperation in this little matter.'

"Lance says, Have your government requested you to say that?

" 'Yes, it have,' the Man says, and he gave us a little exhibition of really first-class coughing. 'Very grateful indeed,' he says, 'and I hope personally that you give our offer some very serious consideration . . .'

"Tooby sure I will, Lance says.

" '. . . for I don't want to think I have just been up here throwing my time away,' Mister Eddie says, puffing on his cigar, 'on account of I am a very busy man. Now I know the price has got to be right and here's what my government are prepared to offer for your cooperation. Mr. Huggins, we got a lifetime position in mind for you. As you may know, the Governor of Puerto Rico has been in office for fifty-six years or more as of this time and I understand he is about ready to retire. How does that appeal to you?'

"How does what appeal to me? Lance says.

" 'Why, the Governorship of Puerto Rico, that's what,' Mister Eddie says. 'We are going to put you in as the next Governor. It's as I said a lifetime position and carries with it some very pretty little emoluments. You get yourself a big house, completely air-conditioned; also a private beach, official car, and not to mention a very comfortable expense account. Also a pension plan.'

"Un-hunh, Lance says.

"Mister Eddie says, 'Then too you got to keep in mind the salubrious climate you will be enjoying down

there. Why, you will never know another unclement
day.' And he looks out the window to call attention to
the weather outdoors; and that sky was nothing to
write home about, let me tell you. 'Horrible,' Mister
Eddie says, and he snuggles down into his overcoat, a
dark job with a velvet collar. 'Horrible weather.'

"Dear old Lance: he sat there so calm and cool,
looking at Mister Eddie, and finally said, Horror and
holiness are the closest of kin in *our* experience.

" 'What's that?' Mister Eddie says. You can imagine his surprise, children; he was really astonished.

"Lance says, If we out-winter this winter, our
hearts will outlast all and every vicissitude.

" 'If,' says Mister Eddie. 'If's a mighty big word
under the circumstances.'

"Mister Eddie, Lance says, we have lived all our
lives in the very center of the great rose of poverty and
we are not going to fink out on account of a little cold
snap.

"Mister Eddie's face turned red; he was all shook
up; you should have seen the way he took on. 'You
people are all alike,' he says, 'ungrateful. Here my
government are offering you a rich plum and you
are rejecting it out of hand. Why, if I was offered a rich
plum like that, you can be sure I'd snap it up real
quick. But what I came up here all this way to discuss,
Mr. Huggins, is *your* problems! You people got a long
row to hoe.'—Children, I'm not making it up: *you
people* is what the Man said, that is exactly the phrase
he used. He says, 'You people don't have pork chop

number one and the winter isn't hardly begun. What you plan to do if I may ask, Mr. Huggins?'

"Lance says, We will barter . . .

"Mister Eddie butts right in, says, 'You will barter, Mr. Huggins?' Oh he came on like he was so stunned it was a shame. 'Mr. Huggins, you know and I know that you don't have the financial wherewithal to barter *with!*'

"Old Lance leans toward him, he leans way over in Mister Eddie's direction, both hands flat on his desk top, says, Mister Eddie, says, we will barter our *poverty,* yes and in places where the dollar ain't king we will find takers.

"Happiness fell down on me when I heard those ringing words. Legions of light walked right in and lit up the dark corridors, let me tell you. It was rewarding.

"And Mister Eddie, poor soul, he didn't know what to say and merely sat there thunderstruck.

"Lance hit him again, said, Baby, I'm the trade you've been plying and now you immoralized people feel lost without me, don't you? We may be a little hungry, Mr. Ambassador, but it is as nothing compared to the hunger and thirst you are going to feel. I feel for you, Mister Eddie, Lance says, I feel for you. And I *fear* for you! Wandering around out there in that forest of contradictions which you inhabit and in which you have lost the way. Et cetera.

"Children, in my estimation Lance could talk just as good off the cuff as on it. You would have marveled if you had ever heard him.

"Well, finally, Mister Eddie picks up his little suitcase, you know, like he has decided not to stay, and he says, 'I am truly sorry for you and your people, Mr. Huggins. Feeling sorry is one of the pillars of western civilization, we go in for it in a big way, and I do feel sorry for you and your people. Sooner or later, you know, you people are going to have to *surrender*.'

"Oh my, you should have seen old Lance flare up when he heard that word; I mean he really reared back and got up on his hind legs. Surrender! he says. Surrender! There is only one thing and one thing only to which we will surrender and we have already done so. We have surrendered absolutely to our fate which is freedom! Let me give you the word, Mister Eddie, he says, let me lay on the scene for you: we had this secret space in us and now we have located it geographically and made it public for all the world to see. It's no secret anymore, baby: freedom was living in us, in that secret place.

"Mister Eddie said, 'I'm on record as being in favor of freedom and the whole world knows it!'

"Well, you can imagine. Lance just threw in the towel for he knew he wasn't getting through; the Man would not let him through. So Lance simply said to Mister E, said, I'm tired, baby, I am so tired, on account of we have been trying to force an echo from you for all too long. Just one final word, Lance says; one word and it is this: When we pulled out we took the mortar with us and now your house is going to come falling down around your ears.

"Mister E is on his feet and anxious to cut out,

knowing he was not going to get what he came for; says, 'I'm going to give you some time to mull over our little offer, Mr. Huggins,' he says.

"But Lance was not finished and had a few more words for good measure, which were: And what's more, Mister Eddie, we do not any longer even care. *Let* the house come falling down!

"Mister E came on like he didn't even hear it. 'No hurry,' he says. 'You don't have to make a decision now. Think about it. Talk it over with the little woman. It's the kind of opportunity comes once in a lifetime. Now suppose we get together next Saturday afternoon and you can give me your thinking on it. I could be back up here around four,' he concluded.

"Lance simply shook his head. I'm issuing instructions to my Minister of Defense right now, he says. I'm issuing instructions to keep you out. We don't want you up here anymore bugging our children with your self-righteousness.

"Mister Eddie says, 'You mean that's your final word?'

"That's my final word, baby, Lance says.

" 'Well, in that case I don't mind telling you, Huggins, I feel sorry for you. You're cold and hungry and your people are cold and hungry and it looks to me you're going to stay that way for a while longer.'

"Lance laughed at him. Yes, Lance laughed at him, he did; laughed and stretched out his arms like he was going to hug the man. Mister Eddie, he says, Mister Eddie, it's cold and it's rough—it's really rough —but to be here is magnificent!"

SEVEN

Yes, children, Miss Brindle was in the rule of her love and you know how people talk. It was beginning to get noised about the town; the word was out. You saw what occurred in Miss Brune's bar and grill. For a kid like me, such as I was then, that was hard to take, let me tell you; hard as salt. For remember that I was still boyish in my thinking and all I really knew of the opposite sex was that my Mother was a woman sure to me. I was really disturbed, and that's a feeling I do despise.

"Scandal was afoot; some citizens hardly talked of nothing else and maybe it was a good thing for it took their minds off the fact that we were still at the place where it was hard times. And I mean the weather, which was really chill, and I mean the rationing, and I mean the peculiar nocturnal activities which were just getting their beginnings around that time.

"Miss Susan Brune, Lance's ex, wrote a new tune for the occasion. I have told you that she had a touch of bitterness about the whole thing. At her club she took to singing a number called *There never was a doctor who could cure their kind of fever*. You couldn't call it kind, but it was a matchless song and one of the best. Remind me and I'll sing it for you sometime.

"Misease came upon us all who were in the circle around Lance. We knew this thing could do him damage and we were all torn up over what to do about it. Some suggested, 'We got to tell Lance what the story is.' And others said, 'No! We got to protect him from all and every sign of it; his mind's got to be kept clear for freedom!' Et cetera and so on. Oh there was all kind of hemming and hawing over this case, and I was just a mere lad and got swayed by every wind. Your minds would have been swayed too if you had heard the wide variety of opinions on this subject. It was enough to run a person insane.

"Yes, Crystal was in the rule of her love alright; and poor Art Rustram he loved her out of measure. His heart was turned. Every time I saw him I marveled at what love can do to a man, and my heart would begin to fail at the thought of their doing something foolish. I got all tired out at the thought of how much we now had to lose. Children, let me tell you, it's always a long hard way when you're traveling to a good place.

"One day I was standing at my post just outside of Lance's private office and I saw Art stealing out of the First Lady's suite. Josea Boutwell, another young-ster just coming up in those days and well known to you from your history books, entered the corridor at the very same moment. Josea stood next to my left side and watched Art move off down the corridor. I turned my eyes away; and I heard Josea say, 'With treason are we waited.'

"He took it hard, Josea did, my yes, for he loved them both, Lance and Art Rustram too, they were dear to him.

"He said to me, 'Brother, I feel like sending out for some bottled beer and high-tension whiskey and forget the memory of the entire thing for one night and a day at least.'

"Children, I knew just what he meant; and all members of the Guard felt the same way too. When duty was over we'd proceed directly to Miss Brune's bar and grill and there they treated us royally. Our money was counterfeit up there and they spread a really nice table for us. Miss Brune used to say, 'You know that you boys in the service always will have carte noire around here.'

"In those dark days—I'm telling you the natural facts now—we'd monkey around at the bar and grill until the wee hours, till we reached the point where you could say, 'Oh it's too sweet to die.' Meaning life, meaning life's too sweet and never mind the darkness of the day you can't let life quit on you.

"The captain of the Guard at that period of which I'm now projecting the tale was Stack Purdy, a really swell fella and loyal from head to toe. He had fought so long and hard for freedom and had received so many non-violent knocks that people used to say, 'It's a wonder he isn't dead.' Not Stack Purdy. Your history book hardly mention his name but thanks are due to Stack Purdy; no use of talking, he was a man who just wouldn't quit.

"I have to confess it, children, that all this gaiety was just for show. We'd laugh it up at Miss Brune's till all hours, but we had a grave-digging feeling in our hearts and no amount of beer could cover it up. It just would not be put down that way. This trouble was shortening down our days and we all knew it and nobody knew what in this everyday world to do about it. I was all confused; I felt like walking and I felt like lying down; I was hungry from head to foot and yet I could not eat; I'd take out my Elgin, look directly at the time, and never even see it. I had an aching heart, that's all I know.

"Miss Brune was full of anger and she got worse all the time. We'd be sitting there in the bar and grill, we would have just about reached the point where we were beginning to feel good. And out she'd come, spotlight hit her, and she'd sing something like, *If you go through here you better walk right;* and we all knew to what she was alluding, and to whom. Yes, it was Crystal she had on her mind. She gave a special significance to her words and when she was feeling really mean, she would growl it out in that special way she had, such as when she sang, *If that's your man, pin him to your side.*

"Some say Miss Susan Brune was hard and malicious, and maybe she was, maybe that's all true; but let's not forget that she was a leading citizen of our new land, and a patriot, and loyal to a T. This thing had shook her up something awful for she knew that the eyes of the whole world were upon us, watching every move we made. Which made it all the more harder to take. I knew the question which was bugging her, for it was the same question bugging me: when would old Lance make his move? Lance knows everything, I said to myself, and he must know this also, I said.

"But I'll say no more now for the moment touching on Art and Miss Crystal and say somewhat about the nocturnal activities which were starting up along about this time. Oh it was terrible. Some citizens said it was on account of the bad actions of Art and Miss Brindle; their love had put us in jeopardy and we had to atone for it. If that's true and I'm not sure it is, then the punishment didn't fit the crime. Well, that wasn't news to us. Anyway, whoever said love's a crime? Show me the man and I'll run him down, I really will. And besides all that, the way the Majority People came down on us at that time, it was no remedy, not for love or anything.

"The Majority People were at the place where they didn't know what to do anymore or how to deal with us. Mister Eddie had come and gone and he went away emptyhanded. They could not buy us and they could not starve us out. Lance warned us; he was always saying, Action brings reaction; we got to be on guard, he says. Says, They're out there in the iron cage plotting the next attack on our sovereignty.

"Lance had predicted it and the day prefixed now came. You should have heard their Radio Free Harlem, you should have seen their newspaper headlines: HARLEM A JUNGLE, MUGGINGS AND MURDERS, HUGGINS UNABLE TO PROTECT HIS PEOPLE, et cetera and so on. The Majority People were getting ready to step in. Lance got on the radio and made one of the most powerful chats I have ever heard in my natural life. Says, They are preparing the ground for invasion, says, and they will come bearing those soiled and tattered banners which read: *We Are Doing This for Their Own Good.*

"Well, we did what we could, all that we were able. At the frontiers the barricades were reinforced with Fifth Avenue buses which had conked out for good and all, given up the ghost and were good for nothing; and the border guard was doubled. Also in the subway checkpoints, because there was talk that they were coming through the IRT tunnel; and we had patrols in the streets all night long. But it availed us nothing. Every morning there was that sad sad business of counting the bodies. My it was terrible.

"I mean we were really up against it. The streets after dark were as unsafe as they could be. People took to staying in their rooms again, watching the teevee. Morale really took a nose dive, I have to confess. And even the rooms weren't safe anymore. They got in everywhere. Within a while there was a lot of mistrust around and some citizens began to say, 'It's

that wild element doing this damage and they ought to
be weeded out.'

"Bad news is soon told, children. It was no wild
element of ours that did the original damage, no; for
they had gone to ground or turned sweet and joined
the militia. But they rose up again at this time of
Lance's temporary weakness. Yes, I am talking about
the Tribal People as they called themselves; the ones
who in the bad old days set themselves up as the
scourge of the Majority People. They would beat up
and were sometimes known to kill any white man
walking on the streets of Harlem; taught themselves
Karate on the rooftops and sharpened their knives.
They thought you could cut your way to freedom, or
talk yourself into it by throwing around such language
as *blue-eyed devils* and *white dogs*.

"Unfreedom had made them desperate. They'd
go for broke at the drop of a hat and thought they
could knock this globe cranksided with their anger
alone. There weren't ever a whole lot of them, but you
only need a hundred or maybe less to unloose terror.
Reason runs. That gave them the advantage of the
grip, you know.

"So when the nocturnal activities started up it
wasn't long thereafter before the Tribal People showed
their hand. They put out the word: For every one of
ours killed, they'd put away a white man. And there
were a few still in Harlem, maybe five hundred, maybe
a thousand. I'm not talking about the criminal element, no; for they were rounded up and deported fast
in the very first days. No, I'm talking about heads of

families, I'm talking about those upright few who had thrown in their lot with us in the old days and stayed on as citizens of the new.

"Here is the bad news. Here it comes. The Tribals meant what they said. On the second day of the Time of the Bad Nights we found the bodies of two white men: an old fruit peddler with a family of six youngsters, and a former Hungarian refugee. And it continued in the same way for five days straight—it was terrible—and Lance only finally stopped it by putting all the whites in protective custody at a secret place where the best of care and consideration was dispensed.

"It was a power play and Lance was in the middle, Majority People pressing him close on one side, Tribals bearing down on the other. Freedom was on the ropes, breathing hard but still hanging on. We walked around like we were treading on cockleburs, I don't mind telling you.

"Bad dreams became the prevalent kind during that period. Old superstitions took over and there was a big run on magic tea and the Gypsies set up in business again. The cult people rose up once more and held a public meeting in Harlem Plaza to clean out the evil spirits; they said the great Raz was angry with us, or somebody like that, I never paid them too much attention personally. But a lot of other citizens who weren't too firm in their faith did so, and the Raz people built up quite a following for a short while there. Every day at sundown they'd come marching

along 125th Street, banging drums and sprinkling
water. I was sorry to see it.

"Some citizens said it ought to be stopped but
Lance wasn't having any of that. He said, Religion is
religion and who is to say which one is better than
another.

"One day along in this time some leading Methodists came to Lance and they had a petition with
them. I showed them into Lance's office and they put it
to him, straight out. They came at the right time for
their purposes because right outside and below
Lance's windows the cult people were marching
around, shouting, 'Purify yourself! Great Raz says
purify yourselves! Destruction coming otherwise!' Et
cetera.

"The Methodist reverends say to Lance, say,
'Brother, how long? How long you going to tolerate
that unholy display?'

"Lance simply says, Freedom of religion is rife
up here; always has been, always will be.

" 'Our God is one God,' this Methodist says.

"So is theirs, Lance replied, and he just stopped
that reverend in his tracks. And meanwhile the cult
people beat their drums and smote pieces of wood and
oh it was eerie.

" 'Listen to that,' the reverend says. 'Why it's
giving us a black eye in the eyes of the whole civilized
western world.'

"The civilized western world can go and catch
itself some air, Lance said, or words to that effect.

"Oh those Methodists, you should have seen

them, they could not abide it; they were getting jumpy. One of them, his shoulders all slumped over and he shook his head; you could see he was all torn up inside. Finally he says to Lance, 'Brother,' says, 'brother, we been almost a year now in freedom, right?'

"Right, Lance simply says, it's getting on for a year.

"The reverend then says, 'It was beautiful. It was a beautiful year, brother. We had a beautiful thing going for us, right?'

"Right, Lance says. Tooby sure we *have*.

" 'Well, Lance brother, what has happened to all that beauty?' the reverend says. 'It does seem to me that beauty has fled and pride taken the day.'

"Oh my, I says to myself, for I could see the writing on the wall; I knew what was coming and I knew I wasn't going to like it one bit.

"The reverend gentleman went on, says, 'Drums beating in Harlem Plaza and murderers roaming the streets at night, people not safe in their houses anymore; nightmares rife all over the land and our Puerto Rican brothers reverting to their Indian gods; funeral processions clogging the streets by day, bodies of innocent citizens sacrificed on the altar of *pride*,' says.

"Watch out now, I said to myself. I felt sorry for Lance; he was looking so sad.

"Reverend says, 'What's happening, Lance brother? Something has sullied the limpid pool of our freedom, that's my feeling on the matter.' And so on; you know how they talk.

"And you should have seen the look on Lance's

face. He was really up tight. He had the look on his face of a man who thinks all his work has been in vain.

" 'What's happening, brother?' the reverend says. 'Do you know or don't you know?' the gentleman suggested.

"Drums beating outside his windows and Lance worried in his heart; I tell you that was one sad scene and my left side was jumping. Finally the reverend gentlemen got up to leave. They saw they had to go away with empty hands and they were ready to cut out and return to their flocks. I felt sorry for them. All they could do was shake their heads.

"But make no mistake, children, they had got to Lance; I could see it on his face; sadness had jumped on him and I was praying it would soon turn go.

"And it wasn't a minute later that Lance shook it off; he stood up and walked to the window and he looked directly out. There below were the original holiness people, banging their drums and sprinkling the purifying water.

"The Methodist gentlemen had reached the door; one of them turned around and said to Lance, 'Yes, brother, it is a sad sad scene to witness,' said.

"Children, Lance turned around right then and there and gave them his famous look. Said, Brothers, I am *with* those people down there!

"General consternation was the rule at that moment. My, you should have witnessed those Methodist faces! Yes, Lance says, and you should be with them too. For they are god-seekers and it was through the search for god, Lance says, that we discovered freedom. He says, We are children of the historical process and one day we are going to emerge on the other side of freedom, in a realm that is yet to be discovered. Says, If you gentlemen think we are stopping *here* and *now* forever after on and that we have got it made, why then you have just got another think coming.

"I tell you, honey, there was no holding Lance down once he got going and in a little while his words were on everybody's lips. Perfect strangers came up to you on the streets and said, 'You heard the news, brother? I am a child of the historical process. Isn't that just what I was saying all along?' Et cetera.

"Or you would hear someone say, 'Man, don't monkey with me for I am history's child!'

"Yes, it is the truth for sure, Lance made people understand what they were all about; he put words in their mouth and a lot of citizens for the first time in their natural lives learned how to talk. You would have been astonished.

"But wait a minute, children; hold on now, for I am getting the historical facts all mixed up among themselves. Here I am out in the streets when the natural fact is I'm still right there in Lance's private office, and the Methodists have all cut out now, and silence reigns supreme.

"Lance is slumped down in his chair. I took one look at him and boyish as I was and young to a fault I knew that he knew. Why was I so astonished? Man, why are you so stunned? I simply asked myself. He knows everything so why shouldn't he know this? I was dismayed, I don't mind telling you. Sadness was on him; for though Art was dear to everyone, to Lance he was dearest, like a son. I looked at dear old Lance and my heart went right out to him.

"I never shall forget it; no, no matter how long I live, I never shall. He looked up at me where I was standing by the door, and he says, What do you think, brother, and has beauty all fled like that Methodist said?

"I was struck dumb! I couldn't get out word number one! I was afraid of what my mouth might utter. Look out now! I said to myself.

"Lance went to the window. Drums still beating, banging away out there in the Plaza. My head was full of them and I wished they'd quit. 'Purify yourselves! Purify yourselves!' the holiness people were shouting. We could hear it loud and clear and Lance must have thought there was a hell hound on his trail. 'Atone! Atone!' the Raz people shouted; I mean they really belted it out. And the look on Lance's face—it was really ruining my heart to see it.

"Lance shook his head; he shook it hard like a fighter coming up at the count of nine. I saw that he could not abide it much longer. He did not look directly at me but spoke his thoughts aloud, said, Is man unequal to manhood? Then he walked back to his desk, slumped down in his chair, and spoke again, saying, We get such love as we deserve. And he repeated it: We get such love as we deserve.

"Oh yes, children, when it came to greatness Lance overlorded us all, but he was human too."

Then the old man fell silent.

Sekou said, "I guess it was along about here that he sent for Art Rustram."

"Tooby sure he did, honey, that's exactly what he did; and if you're good children, I'll tell you all about it tomorrow, for right now I am too sad to go on, thinking about how close we came to nearly losing all we had."

EIGHT

Now unless I'm running into some mistakes," the old gentleman said, lighting his pipe, "unless I'm really running into some, we are now projecting the tale of the time that is known as the Time of the Bad Nights. Now what did I tell you up to now?—Didn't I tell you about old Lance and the Methodists? About Raz and the purification people? And didn't I touch on the matter of Lance's sadness?—All right. Then what am I up to?"

Sekou said, "You're up to the point where Lance is going to say, Find me Art Rustram and bring him here."

The old gentleman nodded. "Well, children, there was yours truly, gun in hand at Lance's office door, at my post and trying to console my mind after being witness to that sad sad scene I alluded to yesterday. I had the feeling, I had the awful feeling that where freedom was concerned, the light was still there but the vision was missing. And that's the reason why my heart began to fail.

"Lance was sitting at his desk. He was in a reverie and he reminded me of a prophet of old waiting for a sign. Suddenly he turns to me and he says, Brother, he says, go find Art Rustram and bring him here to me."

"Oh oh," Ngomo said.

"Yes and I didn't have to be told twice, honey. I did a really smart about-face and cut out on the double; for Lance was in distress—yes, he had the trouble no man ought to have—and I did not relish being there and seeing it. No one enjoys seeing a good man thrown down, no; and I said, Lord, give this good man a break!

"Then I proceeded, I did not stroll, down the hall to Art's office. He was not there. He was nowhere to be found. He wasn't in his office; he wasn't in the Council Chamber, and he was not in the Great Hall of State. No use of talking, I knew where he was . . ."

"Oh my."

". . . and I went there. My once glad heart was failing but I knew it had to be done and yours truly had the job of doing it, no two ways about it. The door was half open and I could see Miss Brindle, my what a beauty she was, lying on a sofa, a little blue blanket to cover and protect her from the chill. Art sat on a chair at her feet. You should have seen him: young, handsome, and faultlessly dressed.

"And there were tears on Crystal's face; she did not touch them, no, but left them run. Art crossed his long legs. 'Dear Crystal . . .' I heard him say.

"She shook her head and simply said, 'I have betrayed me and I am lost.'

"Art heaved a great sigh. Yes, Black House was a house of sighs during that time I am now alluding to. It was terrible.

" 'I don't know where it has come from,' Crystal continued, 'but I seem to have caught this great desire. Lost,' she says, 'lost is what I am, baby.'

" 'Get a hold of yourself, dear Crystal,' Art says.

"And Miss Brindle smiled through her tears and took her bare foot out from under the cover and touched Art's knee with her toe, saying, 'You won't do right yourself, dear, how you want me to do right?' Or words to that effect.

"Art merely sighed again. And Miss Brindle—oh children, when she died I mourned for months on end —she says, 'I have always strived to do right and be right, just as near as I possibly could, considering I was raised in the lap of luxury.'

" 'No doubt about it, Crystal,' Art Rustram says, 'you had a bad start in life.'

"She says, 'Never did I think the day would come that would find me eating acorn soup and soy bean cakes. That's what I had for lunch today and it looks like tomorrow's going to be the same old way.'

" 'We'll pull through,' Art replies, 'you see if we don't.'

" 'Famine,' Miss Brindle says. 'Why it is like the dear old Middle Ages or some other antique times. One never had occasion to use the word over in Teaneck, New Jersey, where I was born and bred.'

" 'Your former life did not prepare you for freedom and its hardships,' Art says to her. 'The suburbs never do and that's a hard fact.'

" 'I'm somehow glad of that,' she says, and she sighed her poor heart out as she said it, 'for if I give my time to thoughts of hunger and food, maybe then I'll be able to wear you off my mind.'

" 'Oh my dear,' Art says, and you could see he had got the agony bad. He threw himself down beside her, kneeling on the cold floor, and put his arms around her like a circle around the sun. Says, 'Crystal, dearest, this can't go on, for if it goes on much longer we will do something careless, foolish, and wild. We got to control our minds because our people now stand to lose too much.'

"Miss Crystal she strokes his hair and smiles, says, 'Dearest, when I'm all alone at midnight I think that way too and I want to go right. But in daylight when I see you, all my good resolutions flee.'

"Well, they enjoyed each other's presence in silence for a while there and I decided now was the time to knock on the door and break it up, and as I was about to do just that I heard Art say, 'The only insurance for us, dear, is that I should go away. I must choose exile and I been thinking of asking Lance to send me on an embassy abroad, to dear old Ghana, Nigeria, or one of the other home countries.'

"Miss Crystal sat up like a shot and put a hand to her little heart. 'Art,' she says, 'if you went away, I would die in a year. I know I could not find the way to live without the solace of seeing you.' She touched him with her hand, touched him on the arm and simply said, 'I desire the evil thing.'

"Well, I could tarry no longer there at the door; I knocked and pushed it a further way open, pretending I had just appeared on the scene, and told Art that Lance was wanting to see him on a matter of important business of state. Miss Brindle turned her face to the wall, thinking to spare me the sight of her tears, I guess, poor girl. My boyish heart was breaking for them; I was torn every whichaway. My heart struck sorrow at the thought of Art, for next to Lance he was the most famous, and he was throwing his life away.

"We walked down the corridor together; yes, Art Rustram himself and yours truly; and I tried to think of something to chat or gossip of but I couldn't think of a thing. Nothing came to mind. Finally it was Art who spoke, and he wasn't hardly speaking to me. He said, 'Before this time another month I may be far far from here.'

" 'That so?' I said.

"And, children, I have the feeling—well, it's just a feeling, you know—that Art wanted to say more and reveal his heart altogether. Men are strange natured that way, you know.

"But all he said was, 'What has Lance got on his mind?' he asked, knowing how close I was to Lance and all.

"I did not want to make Art any alarms so I simply said I did not know; and by then we were entering Lance's private office anyway. He looked up from his reverie, Lance did, looked directly at Art and then looked away. Have a chair, he says to Art; and, Art, he says, I'm a little worried. I am halfway worried that we have allowed this bad situation to advance too far and get out of hand. *Action* is the number for today, Art, he says.

"Well, children, you should have seen poor Art's face. He thought someone had tipped off old Lance, put a bug in his ear, you know; and I could see by Art's face that the panic was on. But he kept himself in strict outward control and said, 'That so?' or words to that effect.

"Yes, Lance replies, doubling the border guards and sending out night patrols have done no good at all; no, no good at all.

"Art sighed with relief and wiped his brow, cold as it was. 'You are right about that, Uncle,' he says, 'other means have got to be found.'

"Lance says, I never have believed and never will that it is any of our own people. This is a move, he says, from the outside in.

" 'No doubt about it, Uncle Lance,' says Art. 'It's a reign of terror and the trade mark of the Privileged People is on it.'

"Too true, Lance says, nodding his head in that famous way he had and crossing his arms at the same time; he was noted for that. Too true, nephew, he says, they are throwing rocks and hiding their hands. Art, he says, we got to break up this thing.

" 'I am at your service,' Art replied, and that simple statement did my heart a world of good, I don't mind telling you. It was cheering, it really was.

"Lance says, Art, I don't want to make you any bad alarms but I must confess there's danger in my plan.

" 'So much the better,' Art says. 'Danger is what I crave right now at this period,' he openly suggested.

"Art was a man of action and, don't forget, he had been hung up for a long time. That plus other reasons which I won't dwell on now made him eager to go and eager to do.

"Art, Lance says, I want nothing less than this and here are my orders: Go fetch me a murderer and bring him back alive.

"Art got the picture right away and nodded his head just once and in the coolest way. 'He'll sing,' he says, 'that type always do.'

"Tooby sure they do, Lance says, and he laid out the plan of action for Art. Art, he says, here's a sad warning: you are going to be nothing but a sitting duck. I want you to pick two picked men and take off, go out in the streets after midnight and make yourself available to death. Hide your men, expose yourself, and let come what may come, Lance says.

" 'I'll take Stack Purdy and this good lad here,' he says, pointing to yours truly. I slapped my rifle with the flat of my hand to salute the man and display my keenness for action.

" 'We start tonight then,' Art says, just as cool as you please for he was already the Art Rustram of old. 'And every night thereafter till we bring you back a murderer.'

"Yes, Lance says, and he's talking as if he's already far far away from us and in another world. Yes, he says, this bad business been going on for far too long already and we got to get quit of it.

"Oh oh, I says to myself, for now I was confused, all confused in mind and did not know which business Lance was talking of and did not know anymore if Lance knew what the true story was. And whatsmore we never did, never did know, although Lance was our brother, the closest kin I personally ever had, but there are some things you don't talk about even to your own brother.

"I decided once and for all that Lance chose Art for the job because Art was the best man for it, a real fighter and with a lot of experience. And then I gave up thinking about it and puzzling it over; had to, for to think about it anymore would have run me insane. I gave it up and turned to action. I consoled my mind with danger. I did not hesitate, children, for if you can't take a step for freedom you might as well be dead.

"And I was hot to walk right through it, walk through freedom to the very edge and out the other side. As Lance told the Methodists that day so long ago. I still grow faint at the thought of what is on the other side and of seeing it at last. As long as I cast a shadow, children, you can be sure that's the direction yours truly will be moving in.

"I will have to continue pursuing this tale tomorrow, children, for it's your bedtime now and I am a little tired myself and I want to be careful not to get the facts mixed up among themselves."

NINE

High living? Nights of forgetfulness at Miss Susan's bar and grill? That was over and finished with and I personally was glad to see the ending of it; for that wasn't gaiety, that was desperation pure and simple. We had just laid around and fooled around in our sorrow, and that's no way for grown men to behave. Now don't get me wrong, I'm not saying anything against Miss Susan Brune or her bar and grill, but that place was a hotbed of loyalty and patriotism, they treated us Guardsmen like heroes, and this gave us a picture of ourselves that was untrue. Things like that going on, some men get the feeling they are hot stuff and the chosen of the earth. But what were we? What were we? I'll tell you what we were: except for Captain Stack Purdy we were youngsters just coming up, still untried and unproven.

"Well, children, here's how it was: once Action became the number for the day, things changed up considerable. Art Rustram, Stack Purdy, and yours truly, we got to be as close as brothers ever get. We shared risk and we shared danger and that brings men really close together, as you know as good as me. We had always called each other brother, true; but it wasn't until the Time of the Bad Nights that we became brothers. I mean we were close, really close.

"Since our work kept us up all night we slept till way up in the day, and this meant that for nearly two weeks I missed my classes up at Columbia U; yes, and those classes were really dear to me. One of the first acts of our new government was to sign what is called a Concordat with Columbia and also with City College, both of which are within our country's boundaries. We gave them permission to continue their good works and in return they provided classes for us in African History and Culture, and other courses of interest to us, as well as library facilities which we needed bad and at least as much as food, as Lance said.

"Some citizens said, 'Lance, you know they are going to infiltrate spies through Columbia and City; don't do it, baby,' et cetera. But Lance simply replied, Education is dear to us and they are going to infiltrate spies anyway.

"You children don't know what it is, I am happy to say, you don't know the thrill of having an armload of books in your arms at the age of fifteen for the first time in your life. I would gladly have given up food, sleep and all to get the learning which I wanted so bad.

"Four months after the founding of Harlem the

first of us started going to college, young men and
women from the militia, and yours truly among them.
I enrolled in the classes of African History and The
History of Revolutions from George Washington to
Fidel Castro. Ask me anything and I'll give you the
particulars including the date. When it comes to
people like Danton, Robespierre, and Camillo Cien-
fuegos, I can tell you their lives and actions to a T. I
mean I really know my stuff in that regard.

"Well, you should have seen the faces of those
Privileged People's students that first day we walked in
to Columbia U. The absence of black must have been
bugging them something awful, and when we entered
in our uniforms they gave us a big hand and a warm
welcome, for you know how youth are. Being members of the exploitative Western Civilization had not
taken its toll of their consciences yet; I mean they were
still striving to be good and their hands were not yet
red.

"Before the week was out some of them were
asking could they come over and join the militia. I had
to tell them we had all the people we could use; I was
polite about it, you know, but I let them know which
way the wind was blowing. They were young and my
they did get upset. 'I'm going to leave this country
before I go insane,' one of them said to me; and I
believe it. I believe it for there are decent people
everywhere and those who lived within the iron cage
were having a really rough time. They could not stand
to see what was happening and worried how it was all
going to end. They looked over the wall at us in our

freedom and they were full of a longing. Like those youth at Columbia U, they were saying, 'My home's not here, it's up there with you.'

'No, children, they are not all devils; some of them are really men and love freedom as we do up here. Well, they're living in a country which just can't reach their case anymore and I am sorry for them from my heart, aren't you? Yes, it's unfortunate.

"Now where was I up to?—Columbia U. Columbia U is where I was at and I won't go into all the ramifications but will only tell you one incident. I'll just allude to it briefly, to give you an idea of the conditions up there and how things had run down without us.

"The coaches were desperate. That's a fact. They lacked men. Not a day passed that one of them did not bug our people with offers: 'Come out for the team,' they say, 'and we'll put you in a place where you don't have to worry anymore. You can do yourself a real good deal, fella.' I mean they were really up the creek.

"Things got so bad that Lance had to write a letter to the president of the U. Lance called in Jim Hardison and says, Jim, send off a letter to Columbia U and tell those people once and for all that for now and ever after on our children will run only for themselves. You can't sell us to Mississippi anymore, says, and we're not going to be bought by Princeton or Cornell either. Tell them those days are gone forever, Jim.

"After that the coaches stole away home and tried to make out with the stuff they had. And what they had wasn't very stylish, as we saw for ourselves just two years later. That was when the first summer Olympics was held at our stadium out on Riker's Island. Our youth brought home nearly every laurel there was, for when it comes to style and endurance, our people just can't be beat; I mean we'll take the cake everytime. But it's just as dear old Lance once said, They want us to prove it too many times because they don't really believe it.

"Now what was I telling you? Where was I up to? Am I out on the street with Stack and Art, or where?"

Sekou said, "You have been missing your classes at Columbia U due to the fact that your work kept you up all night and you been sleeping till way up in the day."

"You have really got it, honey," the old man said. "That's just the way it was. Slept till way up in the day, then met in the map room to read the reports of the night before. Art and Stack, and with my help too, we worked it out that the invaders were following a pattern, hitting a certain neighborhood one night and concentrating some other place on the next. The problem was to figure out where they were going to hit, then to be waiting there, and fix them good.

"No use of talking, it was just guess work and for nine nights Stack and I stood by while dear Art Rustram offered himself to the would-be killers. He was the decoy, the sitting duck, just as Lance said he'd be. Art picked a spot, you see, he picked a spot—you following me, honey?—as for example he'd pretend to be all juiced up and with a bottle in his hand he'd flop on some stoop and lay there stoned. I hid myself in the entrance-way above; Stack hid below the stoop, there in the shadows; and all night long we waited and watched and strived never to blink an eye.

"That was the trap. Art Rustram was the bait. Stack and yours truly, we were the teeth, ready to bite any rat that sauntered in.

"Rats was what they were and rats is how they acted. We figured they were tunneling through from the Other Side for we knew they could not get past our lines. What kind of manner of men could they be? That is what we kept asking ourselves. To do the things they did, crawl under the ground, and then kill those who had never raised a hand against them? They were using every trick in the book: strangulation by wire and outright killing with knives and silencer pistol.

"It was our common belief that they were coming through by way of a tunnel. It was a guileful thing and we were really up tight. Before Lance sent the three of us out on that dangerous assignment, our militia people had checked the cellars of all the houses along both frontiers, north and south. We did not find a trace; no, not sign number one. And meanwhile, death stalked the streets by night.

"Come up and sit here beside me, honey, and don't you worry about a thing.

"I will now pursue the tale.

"By the time night would fall on the streets of Harlem you could see no human soul except for the militia patrols, which were out in large numbers; and by the time night fell Art would decide what our area for the night was going to be. Message goes out to militia headquarters; militia told to stay out of there. That neighborhood then was ours, all ours; it was our kingdom for the night. Any intruders came into our sight we'd know they were from the Other Side.

"Too bad for them. They come from the far shore and on bad business they got to take their chances. That was how I reasoned on those terrible dark nights, waiting in some entrance-way, peering into shadows, watching dear Art Rustram offer himself to a bullet or to cold steel. I wasn't a natural warrior like some; no, I had to work myself up to it and let me tell you it took some doing. And I don't mind confessing it.

"I never shall forget those nights. It was around the end of winter but it was still cold—oh that wind from the river—and it was a-drizzling rain. Streets were slick and shiny as mirrors; there were street lights above and street lights below, each one had another mirrored on the shiny street. But it still wasn't light enough, let me tell you. And it was eerie.

"And by that time there were no buses, no public transportation of any kind; they had all broke down and spare parts were unobtainable. Majority People said No to that. Later, of course, our supply system and repair depots got going and friends on the Outside saw to it that we got what we needed. But in those early days of Harlem's first year to which I am now alluding, you had to walk, walk everywhere. Rationing notwithstanding, we became a healthy people; exercise and purpose made us hardy. The Minister of

Health and Welfare had nothing but good to report on that score. Also, everybody trimmed down considerable and heavy-hipped women went completely out of style. Thin but strong—that was the order of the day in those times.

"For my particular use, it could not have made less difference I want to say. I was in love from head to foot with your sainted grandmother and I could not have cared less whether she was on the heavy or the thin side. In those days you would hear any number of men saying things like, 'My woman's a little on the austere side, but what she's got is what it takes.' I personally never went in for that kind of talk and I advise you against it.

"Well, that's enough of this fancy ta-doo stuff. Let's get back to the scene. Now where are we up to now? I have told you about our studies in the map room and all the guess work we put our minds to and about the weather in the streets at that time. Now here's what we'd do.

"We took no chances; we did not take chance number one when there was a question of human life involved, especially a life so precious to us as Art Rustram's. And since we did not know but what these men from the Other Side might not be roaming around by day as well—keeping an eye on things, you know, and spying out the lay of the land—we figured, you see, that they had died their skin and were passing the other way—oh yes, that's been known, that has been known.

"So what we'd do we'd dress up carefully in

clothes of a nondescript nature; I mean suits that were neither here nor there. We could have been anything at all, representing any calling from the lower ranks of life's various callings and professions.

"So around ten o'clock at night we'd slip out the back door of headquarters and stroll to the neighborhood of our choice, rain falling on us, chatting about this and that in a friendly fashion, with yours truly striving in the worst way to hush the banging of my heart. I tell you, children, after the seventh night of nights like that my nerves were beginning to weaken down.

"We'd wander through the chosen neighborhood until we found some likely place: some stoop or the doorway of a store such as a hardware store, and Art would say, 'This looks good to me, brothers.' Then he'd point out Stack's post and mine, where we were to lie in wait.

"We marked the spot in our minds, never stopping, no, not for a minute, for that would have given the game away and we were taking no chances. Then we'd continue strolling and by this time, it being around eleven o'clock, we'd repair to some local bar and grill, pretending we were after beer and a quiet corner.

"During that period which I am now touching on, most bars and grills were closed up tight by nightfall, due to a combination of two circumstances: a lack of beer, which was rationed, and a lack of customers, most people not finding the streets very inviting at that time.

"Many nights we'd be the only customers present after eleven o'clock, the others having retired to their rooms and their teevees. It was awful the way the citizens hurried home—I mean they did not stroll—to chain and double-lock their doors. I tell you it did our hearts no good at all to see that happening, for it meant we were no longer in control. Come night, and we lost our edge. We were soldiers, Guardsmen at that, vanguard of the Army of Harlem, and we knew what this meant.

"What did it mean? I'll tell you what it meant. It meant the government did not have the power to protect our citizens. The Majority People were just waiting for an excuse like that so as to step in and try to take over. Show me a government that can't protect its own and I'll show you a government that don't deserve to be up there. No two ways about it.

"As I mentioned, bars were nearly always deserted, juke box all by itself in the corner, and only the three of us to give the place the sound of human voices. Barman unhappy, he was thinking of putting out for home, of cutting out and hitting those streets; and usually he'd decide to sleep on a table and wait for day. It wasn't cowardice, no, but it was the wisdom of fear.

"I remember distinctly this one night, it was on the seventh night of our mission and we had gone to Miss Susan Brune's bar and grill. Picture of Lance over the bar, although he frowned on that kind of display. We are not in the personality game, he always said. You want that kind of contest, he says, you can cast a vote for the Miss Rheingold of your choice. Forlorn juke box in the corner and an austere waitress leaning on the bar.

"She brought us our beer—we always took a table at the window so anyone keeping an eye on us would have no trouble doing so, for we were bait that was eager to be caught—brought us our beer and says to us, she says, 'You must surely be very brave gentlemen indeed, out on nights like this.'

" 'Just foolhardy,' Stack says, giving her the wink.

"Stack watched her go, he watched her walking away, back to her post at the bar. He sighed and said, 'Oh my. I have shot dice in Cuba and I played cards in Spain but I never lost anything until I learned how sweet is womankind.'

"We had a lot of time to while away those nights and Stack Purdy was one of the greatest storytellers I ever had the priviledge to hear. He had been everywhere in the world in his youth as a member of the merchant marine. Once he started telling a story and got the slite of it there was no holding him. He really went.

"He had a way of starting in the middle or some place after the beginning. He'd say, 'She was a worldly woman and if I had been wise, I'd have steered clear of her.'

"Then he would fall silent and just stay that way until someone—usually me, for Art Rustram kept a strict and tight silence in those times; Lord knows what it was, the need to keep his mind on the job at hand or the troubling memory of Crystal pining away at Black House—and yours truly would have to break down and say something like, 'What worldly woman was that, Stack?' or words to that effect.

"And Stack would look up with surprise and say, 'Didn't I ever tell you about the worldly woman I met up with in Port of Spain and nearly burned myself out in the process?'

" 'Why no, Stack,' says I, 'I don't believe you ever have as I remember.'

"And then he'd launch out on the tale and I don't mind telling you, children, he always held me spellbound. Maybe Art listened and maybe he did not; I never could tell. He looked down into his glass of beer as if he was trying to read the future there; or he would look out at the street, at the way it was shining under the lights, so quiet, so deathly still.—You comfortable, honey? Well, snuggle a little closer; that's the way.

"Meanwhile Stack going on about the worldly woman in Port of Spain. 'Never met another soul like her,' he says and went on for an hour to describe her deeds and ways. 'She went for fun in a big way and I asked no questions,' Stack said of her. 'I considered her my little wife and imagine my astonishment, after a month of bliss, when a sailor appeared at the door and took one look and said, *What's this?* Well, she wasn't worldly for nothing, this señorita of mine, and she simply says, It's my business, señor, and not any of yours. And meanwhile I'm judging the distance to the nearest window,' Stack says, 'for if there is one thing I want out of it is the clutches of an irate husband. It is one of the first lessons a sailor learns.'

"Well, children, you can imagine. I tried to kick him under the table. I raised my eyebrows and gave him every sign I could think of. Get off this particular subject, Stack, is what I wanted to tell him, but there seemed no way of making this known to him. He just proceeded on the way he had begun and young as I was it did not take me too long to see he was doing it on purpose, for Art Rustram's benefit purely. And it's for your benefit, boys, that I am repeating all this, for I want no scandal attached to this family's proud name, hear?

"Stack went on, 'I got the picture. She was a married woman and had no business there. My heart welled up when I recalled the facts of the case. She was one of those women; they don't mind marrying but they hate to settle down. I cleared out by way of the window and with only an inch or less to spare. Worldly women have their place, I said to myself, but I got to save this body for the freedom struggle; I am not leaving any body of mine in Port of Spain for a cause such as this one.'

"Well, children, you can imagine. After a remark like that, silence reigned in that particular bar and grill; and I don't know to this day if Art heard word number one of all that.

"We sat there stretching our beers to suit the hour of departure and finally Miss Brune enters from the back and joins us at our table. 'How are you, brothers?' she says, and says to Stack and me, 'You

know, this fella,'—and she nods in Art's direction—
'this fella and I were once related by marriage, weren't
we, Sonny Boy?'

"Art looks up and smiles and nods. 'That's true,'
he says.

" 'A mere boy when I first knew him,' she says,
alluding to Art, right there to his face, 'but even then
he had a lot on the ball. Now I hear he isn't up to
much, as it develops.'

"Art said not a word; he simply looked out the
window, looked out at the night's darkness and
chewed the end of a red swizzle stick which he happened to pick up from the table.

" 'Well, that's how it goes, I guess,' Miss Brune
says, 'some people start out with the very best of
everything and end up nowhere at all. Just blow it all
and land at the bottom.'

"Stack replied, 'Well, I see by my watch that it's
nearly time to go.'

"Miss Brune says, 'I'm just a dispenser of music
and maybe I don't know too much, but sometimes I
look around me and feel like fleeing like that bird to
the mountain. And maybe I'd do it too but I don't
know which way to go.'

" 'Things can't be that bad, honey,' Stack says to
her.

" 'I have a faint idea you know they can be,
dear,' she says to Stack. 'But don't you worry, honey, I
won't give you the reason why without thirty days noti-
fication, for none of us are strong enough to take it
straight.'

"Stack says, 'Sis, I know it's all going to work out and come out right, whatever it is you got on your mind.'

"Miss Brune replied, 'The thing that's bugging me is the same thing bugging you.' She then rose and said a final word to Art Rustram—oh she was hard—she says to him, says, 'You used to be noted more so than anyone excepting Lance; but, baby, where are you now?'

"Art was really upset and we all knew it. Miss Brune turned her back on him and walked away, saying, 'It's a dirty shame things have to be this way.'

"Art held his tongue; he sat there like a statue of marble stone, no movement in him. Stack said, 'Well. . .' and he looked out the window; and I personally did not know what in the world to do or which way to turn my face. And finally it was Art himself who broke the ice; he looked at his watch and said, 'Gentlemen, time; time, gentlemen. Let's move out.' His very words.

"Stack checked the time on his synchronized watch, for in exactly three minutes, no more or less, he and I cut out and follow in Art's steps and fall in at our assigned posts. That austere waitress she opens the door for Art and says, 'I know you're brave but please be careful.' Art had that way with women, there's no use denying, and he did not have to try or do a thing; they'd take one look at his lovely face and they'd want to set him up and put him in a place where he'd never have to work again. He was born that way, I guess, and just could not help himself.

"Well, that's the way it went; it went that way for eight solid nights. Not a nibble and the score going up all the time; I tell you there was no doubt of it: we were temporarily on the losing side. It was awful. Those people sent in from Outside, Lord they were artful; I mean crafty and full of guile. Is what they were, they really were.

"Early morning we'd walk back to headquarters emptyhanded and downcast in spirit. It's something about that time of day, I guess. Also it was something about failure, which we weren't used to anymore. For people as proud as we that was hard to take. We returned in silence, could hear nothing but the sound of our heels on the sidewalk. Art would send up our report: No Dice, or words to that effect. Then we'd turn in, but only to toss and be restless on our bunks, anxious for night and another chance.

"And on the ninth night it came, the big chance for which we had been waiting for through all those lonely cold and miserable nights.

"There was Art Rustram—get the picture now—there was Art, all sprawled out over the stoop, an empty pint near his right side, and singing in a hapless way as some do when they have had far too much. Stack was underneath the steps, standing in the shadow of a column of empty garbage cans, darker of hue than the shadow itself. He was an extra darkness there, a wonder to see.

"And yours truly, where was I? In the vestibule above, no lights, leaning up against the mailboxes, thinking of names. I mean there they were, all those rows of names right behind my shoulder blades, and in my boyish way I imagined those names inhabiting the apartments over my head. I tell you it was something, it really was: whole families worrying their hearts out about the troubles we were having, some of them so sick of soul they thought they heard the sound of the picks tunneling under Harlem. And maybe they could so, I could not say; I never heard it myself but the nights were then so awful quiet that a lot of citizens were certain they really heard it for sure. Well, rumors were rife and that kind of thing has got to be expected.

"Don't you worry, though. For all the imaginings and the worry going on in my head, I was alert, I really was. I knew my duty—we all did in those times when alertness and danger was the order of the day—and needed no reminding, no. I knew we were right down to the nitty gritty, to where it counted, really counted, and I kept my eye directly on Art and was careful not to come too near the glass of the door; for my breath would have got it all steamed up. It was in the month of March I'm talking about now but that's how cold it still was. Talk near a glass and you left a mark. Children, doesn't it seem to you that whenever there's trouble it's winter outside?

"Well, it does seem so to me; and now here it is, I won't keep you waiting any longer. Let me tell you how it went. Before my mind had ever taken it in, children—I mean the sight of him, the would-be murderer now approaching Art's supine form—snuggle closer, honey—I found my hand reaching for the Colt in my belt.

"I was good to go as soon as my mind knew what my body was up to, and I made my move. Yes, it's a funny thing how the human system works. Art had his hand on the murderer's throat and that was the start of the fight. The situation was pretty well in hand as Stack and yours truly snapped the trap shut.

"Old Art says, 'Careful, brothers, let's don't damage our prize.'

"And at that moment—Stack had him in a really waterproof hammerlock and I had just as politely as you please removed the knife from that man's hand— when there was this sound: *snick!*—and Art Rustram turned go his hold on the man and clutched his own side, groaned once, and said, 'Brothers, I believe I'm done for.'

"We had been so busy with the man's knife that we did not foresee trouble from anything else—it was our own fault and bad luck—but those people came over well prepared. He had a revolver in his pocket, a silencer on it, and with it he shot Art through the hip, aiming blind and aiming frantic he found a mark nevertheless. The bullet entered and blood was running down to Art's feet.

"Well, Stack gave the prisoner the finishing crack and there was no need to mix it up any further. The man went down and I kept a very good eye on him, let me tell you, while Stack looked to Art.

" 'Stack, I'm bleeding bad,' I heard Art say; and in all that weather Stack tore off his shirt and stopped up the hole in Art's side. Art said, I could barely hear him, said, 'If I die, don't fault me. I chose but what I must. Tell all my good friends, please, for I have the feeling I won't last long as I'm weak in my limbs and breath.'

"Stack readily consented and furthermore said, 'Don't torment yourself now, brother;' and he signals to me to go and put in the agreed upon call to headquarters. I did so and I did so fast, because I knew by the expression on Art Rustram's face that he must be near to death. I reported to the C.O. direct, said, 'Major, we have got our man and Art's wounded bad,' and told him where to find us.

"I ran all the way back; it was drizzling rain; it was falling like morning dew. I did not lose a second getting there; no, not one. Art was in real pain but he stood it like a man. Says, 'Brothers, I hope the citizens will not think ill of me, for life is not worth living if they do.' He could hardly talk and Stack told him to save himself and be silent. But he went right on, seemed he could not stop himself, said, 'I fear that scandal has damaged my name.'

"Stack says, 'Hush now, brother, you'll be getting the best of care soon,' for we could hear the sirens unwinding, they tore the night apart, I mean they really wailed. First thing we did we got Art in to the ambulance and on his way to Harlem Hospital where the best care in the world is dispensed, western style and acupuncture too. We closed the door to the ambulance and 'Poor boy' said Stack. Then we turned our attentions to the man from the Other Side.

"We put him in the back of the big command car which had been sent for us and Stack propped him up on the seat like a bale of hay and clapped a gang of chains around his wrists. He then whipped out his little old pocket flash and shone it on the prisoner's face.

"You can imagine our astonishment at what we saw! 'I'll be double damned,' Stack simply said and ripped open the man's shirt, saying, 'Just want to see if he's as black underneath as he is outside.'

"There were three militiamen with us plus the man driving and they were all struck by what they saw, believe it. General sadness hit bottom. It was too hard to believe. That man was one of our own, no getting around it, children; he had turned against us and was doing the dirty deeds for the Other Side.

"Stack wrung his hands. He was all shook up. Well, I knew just how he felt. Said, 'Brothers, I have never in my life felt so forlorn,' Stack said.

"I knew it, for I was feeling that way too. I sat there on the jump-seat, I looked at that man's face, and I secretly mourned.

"All this is a great long while back, children, but I remember the feeling as if I felt it only yesterday or no longer than week before last. Along in those times, because of the actions I witnessed and the things I heard, I was one of the saddest persons you would ever want to see. I mean I was really far down for a while there. The thing is, it hits you hardest when you are young at a certain age."

TEN

It is now the next day. Prisoner's in the cooler and my how he did sing. Those types always do. No undue pressure was brought down on him; he was willing and eager: told us everything touching on where the tunnel was, and also how many men had been employed, who trained them, et cetera and so on and on. He incriminated practically the entire human race except only himself, for whom he begged mercy.

"Children, you should have seen that guardroom: militiamen and plain ordinary citizens coming from the length and breadth of Harlem to have a look at that fella. He was of the long slender type and dressed in a one-piece dark green jump-suit. It had the biggest pockets I have ever seen. Well, he needed roomy pockets to carry all the junk they gave him.

"His masters sent him out loaded to the gills. He had a complete drugstore in one of the pockets, including a hypo containing stuff to be used in killing himself painlessly in case of capture. But he wasn't the

125

kind to turn go of life for any principle, for he didn't have any in the first place and was just a businessman engaged in the business of murder. And in his other pocket he carried a complete armory. You should have seen it. It was awesome.

"Oh no doubt about it, he was well equipped in the way of accoutrements, but inside himself he was lacking totally in what it takes. We stripped him down to his skin first of all and examined him every which-awhere for any hidden implements of whatever kind. Then we gave him pants without a belt, not being desirous of taking any chances; shoe laces also, we took them away. Put four men to guard him, two inside the cell, two outside. We cared for him like a baby. He was our prize and he was our evidence.

"Yes, you would have witnessed an astonishing sight if you could have seen how the citizens lined up by the hundreds to get a glimpse of that man. They clamored to see him. It was something. Lance said, Let the people in. And they came every day to take a look and satisfy themselves as to the prisoner's true color.

"I was reminded of this event many years later; something happened then to put me in mind of it and raise it in my recollection. It was twenty years later it occurred, or maybe thirty; I don't remember distinctly —but it was at the time the Privileged People got a hold of a young woman of our race.

"Don't ask me where they found her. Some say she was the daughter of a cook who worked for a family so far out in the suburbs that she never did hear what was going on in Harlem; she didn't receive the call and therefore stayed put and raised her daughter in ignorance. That's the way it must have been.

"Or maybe it was some other way. But the fact is some Privileged hustler discovered her and put that poor child on exhibition. She was at that time going on eighteen years of age as I remember. They put her in a nightclub and charged fancy prices to see her. Majority People came from miles around for a glimpse of the girl; they had not seen skin like that for more years than they could count and they were hungry for the sight of it.

"Proposals of marriage poured in by the dozens; artists painted her; poems were written; and all she did was stand on a revolving stage in a glittery gown that must have cost ten dollars a yard and let them glimpse her beauty while the hustler made his spiel. You'd see her pictures in all the magazines which came in from the Other Side, and in full color, too, saying things like *Miss Milicent's Favorite Perfume Is Lover-Be-Good.* Or they'd have her saying: 'My skin is too delicate for ordinary soaps and that is why I only use *Bland,* the soap of the stars.'

"She just didn't know. Privileged People kept her in a condition of total ignorance; never let her see a newspaper and held her in a gilded cage. It was terrible. She thought she was alone in the world and the only one of her kind. How was she to know? By that time—this was around thirty years after the founding of Harlem—there was not Negro number one left in Manhattan, and elsewhere they were growing rarer every day, some coming to us here and some going to the original home in dear old Africa. I mean the Majority People were in a really bad way when it comes to variety. Sameland the land of Sameness, that is what we came to call it and that is what it is.

"Well, you can imagine; we were stunned for a minute there, but our government soon lodged a strong protest. Old Jim Hardison, he was still alive and kicking, he wrote it and it really wailed. Did no good. No good at all. So we got some friends to put in a complaint at the UN; we took it all the way up to the Human Rights people.

"Mister Eddie's successor at the UN said, 'This is free enterprise at work and an internal matter purely. You tell one hustler what he can and cannot do and you'll have Socialism creeping over the land faster than you can say John Maynard Keynes!'

"Oh dear," Sekou said.

"You said a mouthful, honey," the old gentleman replied. "And poor Miss Milicent—Miss Milicent Hodge was her name now that I come to think of it—she finally died of loneliness before that year was out, and you can't call that a natural death but that is purely what it was: death by loneliness. She pined away for her own kind and never even knew what ailed her. Children, I can't imagine a more miserable way to go than that, can you?

"The thought of that poor girl has bugged me for years. And that hustler would not turn go of her; no, not even after she was dead and gone. Death himself could not soften that man's heart. He had Miss Milicent embalmed; he placed her in a glass case; and he put her on view in a store on Times Square. Fifty cents admission and he's still collecting; parents bringing their children for a look, standing there hushed at the sight of her. Little sign says: *A Negro Woman, Last of her Race to live in Freedom.*"

"Oh my."

"Yes, it's sad but that's how it went and that's how it goes. Now where was I up to?"

"Citizens coming for a glimpse of the prisoner," Diego said.

"From far and wide they came, honey, far and wide; and as the days went by, more and more of the people showed up, and not less and less as you might think. Why was this? I'll tell you why. It was because the citizens of Harlem just could not believe he was one of our own. They believed he had been dyed and that if we kept him in the cooler long enough, he'd fade back to his original whiteness.

"But such was not the case; no, it was not to be.

"And you would hear any number of well-meaning citizens say, 'That poor lad, they must have brainwashed him good.' And other statements to that effect.

"Lance himself came down to the guard room. He took one direct look at the boy and he said, Brothers, I know the type: whiter than white.

"Lance took the tape recording of the prisoner's long confession and he played out the whole spool on radio station WEBDuBois. Afterwards, he made one of the most memorable chats it has ever been my pleasure to hear and you know I have been casting a shadow for a long long time.

"He was in fine voice that night; the people were in the streets again—the tunnel having been found and blocked up—and a general air of jubilation reigned. Since the capture there had not been a single act of violence, except for a neighborly quarrel here and there; but no hand had been raised against another human soul.

"Well, there was Lance at the microphone and there was yours truly, right at his side, back at my old post. Lance was fiddling around with the electric wire in that famous way he had, saying, Brothers and Sisters, you've heard it all and I hope you'll now stop tormenting yourselves, says. This boy is not one of ours, he is one of *theirs*. He is a plastic man! and he was manufactured by the Privileged People!

"And that is how this came to be known as The Time of the Plastic Men. For as Lance said, these men weren't men at all, no; they were products! Products is what they were and they had been made sick to their souls by their mechanical condition. They were wind-up men and they were the last of their kind for we don't breed them like that anymore and the Majority do not have the power to manufacture them anymore.

"So Lance says, Now what are we ever going to do with this boy? Says, We have abolished capital punishment and we are not going to bring it back for *him!* Such barbarities have been banned forever in *this* part of the world, Lance says.—Oh yes, he rubbed it in a little; he took the occasion to give the Majority

People a nudge for their backward ways.—He says, And I see no point in housing and feeding this plastic creature for the rest of his un-natural life.

"So what we going to do? Lance asked the citizens. It beats me, he says. It's a problem and we're just going to have to sit on it for a while. You know, he says, when Napoleon invaded Spain, our Spanish brothers traded French prisoners for pigs. Maybe that's what *we* ought to do, he says, trade this boy for a few tons of the best ham.

"Well, he raised a big laugh with that line but the Majority People took him seriously. Well, you see, that's the whole thing in a nutshell: when we cracked a joke, they never knew to laugh; and when we were dead serious they always thought we were joking. It was a sad sad situation, let me tell you, and no good for anybody's health.

"Mister Tom Man, who was at that time the Majority's president down in Washington, he got on the teevee and said, 'Now naturally the whole world knows we don't have thing number one to do with the recent alleged events up in Harlem; but in accordance with the spirit and letter of our humane traditions, I am going to form a committee of private citizens to raise hams and ransom that poor innocent boy.'

"Mister Tom kept right on saying he did not have a thing to do with the nocturnal activities we had been suffering, and the opposition congressman said, 'Tom honey, we *know* you didn't have a thing to do with it and that your hands are clean but you should have sent in air support.' It was one big mix-up, let me tell you, and there were a lot of red faces down there, as they say.

"Also at the dear old UN there were many friendly countries who got seized by the notion of lending us a helping hand and they came down hard on poor Mister Eddie. Oh my, that boy did more coughing than was good for him; he showed photos of the tunnel and said, 'Look here at this sloppy workmanship; that proves it couldn't have been done by us. We got too much technical know-how to build any tunnel as sloppy as that!'

"So they formed this committee containing a football coach and a retired admiral in the time-honored way, and Lance sent Josea Boutwell to meet with them. Lance picked a number out of a hat in a manner of speaking and said to Josea, Tell those people we want a hundred tons of the best ham in return for that boy of theirs.

"Josea met them at the border and I went along for the ride and to witness history in the making; I had got a taste for it, you know. It was down on Robeson Boulevard, formerly Second Avenue, at the southern frontier, and Josea says to them, 'A hundred tons of Grade A ham and that boy of yours will be delivered whole into your hands.'

"The retired admiral says, 'Now, son, you know that boy ain't none of ours but we just want to do the humane thing.'

" 'Un-hunh,' Josea says.

"Admiral replied, 'Tell you what we'll do, we'll

give you fifty tons. I think that's a very generous offer, son, all things considered.'

" 'I didn't come here to bargain,' Josea says. 'The number is one hundred and if you call me *son* just one more time I will double it.'

"Coach says to the admiral, says, 'Admiral, let's retire to the locker room and talk this over with the alumnae association in a manner of speaking.'

"Coach and the admiral, they step back a little ways behind the barrier and carry on talk of an agitated nature. The admiral got all angerly and we could hear him say, 'I turn the twenty-inch guns on this whole land mass and reduce it to rubble if it wasn't that we owned it all.'

"Coach says, 'We used to, admiral sir, we used to but they broke through our service and nationalized everything we had right down to the cleats in our boots. Now what I say is let's get in there and fight, fight, fight, for the old Statue of Liberty play don't work anymore.'

" 'Why won't that boy let me call him *son?*' admiral says; oh my but he was all agrieved over that. 'I don't know whichaway is up anymore,' admiral says. Says, 'Did you tell these people who I used to be?'

"Coach says, 'Admiral sir, the flying wedge is out, was outlawed since way back and gone. Now let's get out there, play hard and play clean and make them an offer of seventy-five tons.'

" 'I won't give an inch,' admiral says, 'and you

know how dangerous I am when aroused. I wasn't called Bulldog for nothing!'

"Coach takes him by the elbow and leads him back to our lines where Josea Boutwell is smoking a Corona just as cool as can be.

" 'First and three, admiral,' coach says, 'and we're on our own ten, remember that.'

" 'Let's offer them seventy-five,' admiral says.

" 'Good idea,' says coach, fiddling with the whistle around his neck. 'Boutwell,' coach says, 'you got the wind in your favor but I know you are going to play like gentlemen. We're offering seventy-five and I know you'll accept that in the same generous spirit in which it was offered.'

" 'I have got my instructions,' Josea says, 'and I didn't come here to dicker. One hundred is still the number for today.'

"Coach says to the admiral, 'Baby, it's the old squeeze play and good sportsmanship is not to be expected. Why, they ain't even members of the conference.'

"Well, children, I won't keep you waiting; the long and short upshot of it all was that the Privileged People gave what we demanded and delivered one hundred tons of Grade A ham in one week's time. The Great African & Pan-Islamic co-op stores were bulging at the seams. Extra rations were declared and our spirits received a real lift.

"On receipt of the hams we turned over to them the prisoner, all sound of body and limb and broken in spirit; good for nothing. Well, I don't need to tell you, dears, it does not take much to break a plastic man. He covered his face whenever our cameramen strived to get a shot of him; he had just enough humanity left in him to feel a little shame, I guess.

"Our people saw him in the newsreels and some began to feeling sorry for him again, saying things like, 'Well, that boy probably could not help himself,' and 'He must have been thoroughly brainwashed to do a thing like that,' and 'Maybe he had no Mother to guide him.' Et cetera and so on.

"Lance wouldn't hear of it; he wasn't having any of that, no. On his very next radio chat he took the occasion to have the final word on the matter. I'm not telling you to hate that boy, Lance said; no, I am not telling you to do anything of the kind. I'm just telling you how I feel myself, says, and this is the way I feel: if you *force* yourself to love somebody, you give birth to a murderer in your own body!"

"One of Lance's most profound utterances," Sekou said.

"Tooby sure it was, honey," the old gentleman said. "It was a companion utterance to another famous saying of his, I mean the one about anybody walking a mile with a heart full of false sympathy is walking to the funeral of the whole human race."

"It is graven on his statue," Ahmed said.

"You do know your facts, honey," the old man said and prepared to rise from his chair. "Children, right now I am off to the Veterans of the First Day

Lodge. Tomorrow if I'm still casting a shadow I will project the tale of Art Rustram's life and death struggle at Harlem Hospital and of how with the help of others he caught new courage and came back out of death."

ELEVEN

It was a week or more had passed since the Time of the Plastic Men had been brought to an end, and Art Rustram's life was still hanging in the balance and teetering this way and that. The reports from Harlem Hospital were none too good, let me tell you, and all his many friends were worried sick. The doctors let Stack Purdy in to see him and some of us Guardsmen went along; well, imagine our sadness when Stack came out and said, 'That boy seems to have lost the will to live.'

"Sad? I'll tell the world it was. Art Rustram had always been a moody man; brave but moody summed him up to a T. And now his mood turned him to thoughts of death; in his own mind he had turned go from life. Doctors strived to do everything in the world for him but it did not avail anything. His wound refused to heal and he suffered greatly but took it like a man.

"One day Lance himself went to see him, he went to the hospital and yours truly drove him there and waited in the hall outside. What if anything passed between those two, him and Art, we will never know. Lance came out and his face looked like it was carved of marble stone. He got in to the front seat beside me, laid his head back for a minute and closed his eyes. Then he roused himself and sat up straight, said, I can't let myself get tired, brother, for my time is not my own.

"He said, Art must not die.

"Children, it was as if he was making a decision of state, as if he was sitting at his big desk making decisions affecting us all. That is how it seemed to me.

"Then he went on. Ain't our people something? Lance said to me. We really are marvels, he says. Says, Brother, throw your mind back to the freedom struggles and recall how many heroes our people produced from their midst, I mean really genuine heroes. And look at the Majority People with all their superior numbers going for them, he says. And did they put forth a single hero? You know they did not, brother; you know what they came up with: Tom, Dick, and Harry, that's what they came up with.

"Art Rustram is of the company of genuine heroes, Lance says. He must not die!

"No, *sir!* I says. For, children, it was just as if he had given me an order.

"When we got back to Black House, Lance leapt out of the car. I did not have clue number one as to what he was up to, but followed him inside and to my usual post. Youngster on the corner was selling the newspaper, headline read CONDITION CRITICAL. Didn't even have to mention Art's name for everyone knew. People bought the paper and simply shook their heads. Harlem contained a lot of worry along about that time, for Art was well loved and sure to be missed. As Miss Brune rightly said, Next to Lance he was the most famous.

"Thinking about one thing and another and how my ways had changed so drastically, I mean from the ground up, in just six-seven months' time—for that time the year before I was still a resident of dear old Smudgeville—upwards of a good thirty minutes must have passed on and Lance just sitting at his desk, chewing on a paper clip and staring into vacant space.

"Suddenly he got up off his chair and came charging right past me, headed down the corridor towards Miss Crystal's apartment. I high-tailed right after him, which was my job to do, and got there just in time to hear him say, Crystal dear, I must ask your aid.

" 'It's too late now, Lance dear,' I could hear Miss Brindle say. 'It's far too late for I am in such distress. You brought me to this land and it has meant only pain to me, wrested from my kin, here among this strange people.'

"You know me, dear, Lance says, and you know I wouldn't ask you to do anything against your heart.

" 'My heart's been turned since the night I met you,' she says, and I heard her sigh from her heart, 'two years ago, at the Cotillion in Teaneck, before

Harlem ever got started; and I have lived only in your shadow ever since. Oh Lance, dearest, I didn't set out to deceive you, you know. It was only that my nature wanted to discover itself after all those years of unfreedom in Teaneck's comfortable iron cage. Baby, how is it you have never told me off or sent me away after the things I've done to you?'

"There was a little while of silence and then Lance said, You gave me all you had to give me, love; and there were times and I knew it when you did my will despite your desire.

"And Miss Crystal replied, 'I wanted a man who had set all his mind on love, and that was a thing I never could get from you, dear. Freedom was always uppermost with you.' She then cried out, 'Oh it's you who have accomplished my shame!'

"Lance stood for it, children; he took it like a man, yes, he did. Well, what would any of you have done in his place? Tell me if you think I'm wrong and old-fashioned and completely out of date and not seeing freedom from each and every angle as I should —am I wrong?—and that you would have done the same? Well, maybe so; but oh it's very difficult for me, raised as I was on the Baptist side and at that particular time."

The old man sighed, was silent a moment, and then went on with his tale. "Now here we go," he said, "and this is what Crystal said next: 'Oh this sorrow in my life,' she said. 'This heartly sorrow. Hasn't it warred upon my beauty, dear? Tell me do you love me still and find me beautiful?'

"And will for evermore, I heard Lance say.

" 'It seems to have worn me away to the bone,' Miss Crystal says. 'But I'm happy you don't see it, dear, for truly I desire you above all things, and your love.'

"Crystal, Lance says, I have come to ask you a favor.

" 'Yes,' she says, in a sad sad voice, 'I guessed you were here for something of that nature, for I do not see you much otherwise. Alright, honey, tell this spoiled darling what it is you wish.'

"Children, I am now going to cut out all super-fluity," the old gentleman said, "and really get down to it: Lance told Crystal simply this, that he wanted her to go to the hospital and rouse Art Rustram up out of death and bring him around to life again. I have my sorrows too, Lance says to her. I believed the lies in my heart, I heard Lance say; and there's no remedy for it, dear, I'll just have to go on in the same old way.

"And Miss Brindle sighed and tenderly said, 'Then so will I, dear; and you know there isn't any-thing in this world I wouldn't do for you. Give me one kiss and I'll pack a little basket and be on my way.'

"I proceeded halfway back to my post on hearing this and soon Lance showed up and instructed me to get the car and take Miss B to wherever she wanted to go. That is how he put it and I did just that and was sitting in the car waiting for her, at the side door of Black House, and there she comes, Miss Brindle, Crystal herself, all wrapt in furs. Oh the sight of her! She went to my head everytime, believe that. And let's

face it, children, I'd have done anything short of treason for that woman. Well, that's the jeopardy of love,
honey; all the books talk about it and you'll learn it
yourself sooner or later.

"She walked directly to me and got into the car,
carrying a little basket. I didn't have to ask the way; I
headed straight for Harlem Hospital.

" 'I guess you know where I'm going,' Miss B
says to me. 'I'm afraid of hospitals, you know, but
something has given me the courage to go.'

"I strove to reassure her; I said, 'Harlem Hospital
is one of the best and it's freshly repainted and not
scary at all, as hospitals go.'

" 'I'm sure of that,' she replies. 'But it isn't the
place, you know; it's the thing. Death's the thing I
fear; I grow faint in the presence of it, and even at the
very thought.'

"I guess there are a lot of people like that. I said
nothing in reply and before too long, in not more than
a little while, I pulled up and parked, helped Crystal
from the car and took the little basket from her hand.
She did not even seem to know it was there or that I
had taken it; that's how wrought up she was. I mean
she was really all wrought up by this time, she really
was.

"Doctors and nurses they saw who it was and
stepped back along the walls, just simply stood there
and gazed at her as she went by. Oh I tell you, she was
something to see. No, no one could hold a candle to
her, not at that time I'm touching on and so far as I
know not to this very day.

"I showed her the way to Art's room and when we got there I said, 'Honey, this is it; here it is, sis.' She caught some courage then and walked right on through, and yours truly right behind her.

"At first sight of Art Rustram she stopped, and sighed with all her heart; oh my but it was touching. He was all wrapt up in bandages and being fed from a bottle, through a tube, you know, which led directly to his vein. Bubble rising every little while in the bottle and that was the only sign of life; no other indication. Light sifting through the curtain touched poor Art's face and you could see an artery in his forehead. It was throbbing away for dear life.

"And Miss Brindle? She was in a dream, she really was. She did not seem to know where she was going, but headed for Art with her arm outstretched. She looked like she thought the little white chair by his bed was a mile or more away. But she reached it without any mishap nevertheless, and she picked up his free hand and she held it to her face.

" 'My friend and love,' she says—yes, those were her very words she did utter—'I desire to have no other delight than being by your side.'

"Well, children, I do not know what it could have been but a queer feeling came over me, which seemed to say Oh oh, those two are saying their last goodbye. I just stood there for a little while and felt sadness welling up in me; then I remembered myself and who I was and I took the basket and set it on Art's table beside the bed. Crystal did not even see me and I retired to my place at the doorway and sat down behind one of those screens that hospitals always have, for they got to expect the worse it seems.

" 'Crystal.' Yes, it was Art Rustram's voice; it was weak and far-off sounding but I would have known it anywhere. Silence reigned then for a second or more, until Miss Brindle said, 'Yes, friend, we have been dissevered from each other.'

" 'Now you are here,' he says, 'sweet love.'

"She commenced to cry, she cried bitterly; oh her grief was really something to see. Art begged and begged her to stop.

" 'Then come back out of death for me, honey,' she says to him.

" 'No matter, friend,' he says, 'no matter at all; for whether I be quick or dead, you alone are ever in my heart.'

" 'You must not die!' she cried. Lance's very words; and she uttered them in the very same way, as if it was a commandment. *'You must not die!'* Just like that.

" 'Live,' she says, 'oh my dear friend, live and recomfort me somewhat for this grievous life I am having. My foolish heart that was once so gay and light is heavy now.'

" 'It seems we could not avoid to love one another,' Art says; and my there was such heartily sorrow in his voice. My heart welled up to hear it; I tell you, I was close to the breaking point.

"Miss Brindle says, 'Hush now, love, and eat some of this fine soul-food I have brought you. It is of the best.'

" 'No,' says Art, 'I want to proceed on the way I have been going, to meet death which knocks at my heart. I'd rather die deedless than do damage and bring shame on him.'

" 'Live for love of me, love, or else, love, I'm going to die too,' she says, 'believe it.'

"No, my ears did not deceive me; before I knew what for, I heard the sound of silver clinking on a dish, and Miss B saying, 'Yes, there, this will bring you back.' She wept, oh my how she did weep, and her grief had turned into tears of joy for she saw Art Rustram turn go of death and reveal again the will to live.

" 'You are my most solace,' I heard him say. 'I will do what you bid me,' he says, 'even though my ending be a shameful one and I be defamed.'

"She says, 'Sweetheart, that's not the way it's going to be. You have come back from the far shore and old loves are old loves. When you come back fully to life, friend, you will start anew.'

" 'I desire no other,' he says, 'and what's more never shall.'

" 'Baby,' says she, 'you are being reborn. I have got my life and now you must find yours.'

"Young as I was and boyish to the extreme I knew what this signaled. So too did Art. 'Oh Lord,' I heard him say and it struck sorrow to my heart on account of there was so much of loss in it. He knew what the score was, no doubt about it, but he took it like a man. And wasn't she brave? I'll tell the world she was, and don't you ever doubt it.

"Well, Miss B came to see him every day thereafter without fail, bringing him the best that Harlem could afford in the way of food and drink, and in less than a month's time Art Rustram was on his feet again. He looked drawn and he looked sad but he still had that debonair look around him and the nurses couldn't do enough for him. There wasn't one of them who did not want to set him up for life. It was Major Rustram this and Major Rustram that all the way up and down those hospital halls.

"The way things were and I having the inside knowledge I had, I was not astonished one bit when I heard the big news. Yes, it was around this time that Art went off to Africa—he landed up in Ghana appointed roving ambassador there at his own request.

"Children, I'm glad to say I missed the farewell scene, if ever there was one; for I tell you the truth, I don't believe this heart of mine could have stood it."

TWELVE

Except for two events only, about which I have yet to project the tale, I have now just about brought you up to date on Harlem's first year. I won't bother you with the story of the Colored Invasion Army because the history books do up that tale pretty well and you know the facts: how the invaders only got as far as 100th Street and Fifth Avenue, where our militia under the command of Josea Boutwell bottled them up, corded them off, and put them down. We ransomed them out of Harlem in no time at all hardly, and to this day I can't look at a ham without sadness whelming me.

"Let me tell you it was no laughing matter and the going was really rough. We were fighting hand to hand at 98th and Fifth, mortar fire pinning us down, and our women at the windows of the houses cheering us on in the Algerian way.

"And then Stack Purdy led a charge which made the day for us. I remember distinctly we were on an

eastbound street but I don't remember which and
Stack saying, 'Let's roll!' Well, we hit Fifth Avenue
and there I saw our own men all asprawl, lying in their
blood every whichaway. Nothing could stop us then.
Stack yelled, 'Wake up, dead man, and help me drive
my row!' I tell you, children, such was our fervor I
would not have been astonished to see the dead soldiers rise up and follow our charge. Oh we were filled
to the brim with daring and I personally would not
have stopped even if I saw myself dying.

"It was three days like that and my rifle never
left this hand. My hand hasn't got over it yet. It was
not exactly a pleasure, dearies, so don't get any funny
ideas. War's no easy street, I don't care what the
movies say. I'd be sorry from my heart to see that kind
of action ever starting up again. Though I was in my
prime, so much death was a bitter lesson which I have
never forgot; no indeed I have not. And I want to tell
you further that I'll gladly greet the day that brings the
idea of war to a permanent conclusion.

"And as you know this wasn't the last time the
Privileged People strove to break us by means of direct assault. As far as they are officially concerned we
did not exist, but they still wanted to get rid of us in
the worst way. It must be eerie for them, it must upset
their heads, knowing we are here and trying to pretend
we're not. Or I don't know; maybe it's easy for them
once they get used to it. It must be so for otherwise
they'd have recognized us by now and admitted we got
a claim to a piece of this earth, for they always do
what's easiest.

"Well, now that's enough about the war—don't get me started on that scene for the thought of it is enough to run me wild—and besides, that was at the beginning of Harlem's second year and I'm still trying to bring you up to date on our first.

"Yes, it's Miss Brindle for sure; it's her I have in mind, poor soul. She was too sweet to die."

The old man took time to light his pipe; the children watched in silence and waited for him to continue. Finally, Ngomo said, "Fill in the scene for us, grandfather, please."

"I was just about to do that, honey," the old gentleman sad. "I am now about to fill in the scene for you. Miss Brindle had done her duty and she had brought Art Rustram out of death; he, when he recovered completely and was back in top-notch condition, he went off to Africa to make treaties and other things in that line. He became a permanent fixture over there and came home to Harlem only many years later, when he knew it was time for him to say farewell to this workaday world of ours.

"And Lance, he was busy night and day striving to get us out of our unfinancial condition, borrowing change from this country and that, which is called the business of state. And when it came to foreign relations, Lance was tops, believe it.

"Well, that's how it was. Art had broke the ice and gone, Miss B's world was shook to its very joists, and Lance was up to his ears in work.

"Children, it did not take long. After just a little while Miss Crystal took to her bed and began to pine, told the doctor, 'Doctor, I have this burning seems to burn me here.' It was around the place where her heart was.

" 'She got a little fever is all,' the doctor says. How was he to know? That doctor was no fool but he just did not know that Crystal's heart was ruined. She loved Lance, she loved him clean through and he was as good as a man can be. Then she had her loving fun and now she could not get it out of her mind.

"That was the situation, bad enough to begin with and only worse was to follow, and the time wasn't long when it did so.

"Crystal lost nearly all the looks she ever had; I mean, children, it was still there, the beauty, oh my yes, she was still touched with it, but now it was all clouded over with sadness and from gold she turned to ashy grey.

"She was sick to her soul was what it was, the cause of it, and her upbringing was against her as Art had said. It did not give her the strength, which was what we needed plenty of in those times. Touching on Miss Brindle I would say that she was a tree all loaded down; that is what I would say, yes.

"She took to wandering the halls at night in her long lacy gowns—she had brought all that from Teaneck, New Jersey—and with a green wool shawl around her shoulders for protection of the cold. The natural fact is, she was looking for something; no doubt of that, I have no doubt of it personally.

"She got unconnected. It's a too too common thing in a situation such as hers and I would ofttimes

come upon her in the wee hours of the morning—
yours truly by this time was sergeant of the guard and
had pretty much of the run of the place; besides which
my duties took me to every nook and cranny, including cellar and roof—and I would come upon her,
her one hand clutching the shawl together and her
mouth tight with looking.

" 'Brother,' she says to me this one time I particularly have in mind, 'brother, not one single letter has
he written; no, not even a line. If his heart's not iron, it
must be marble stone.'

"I led her gently back to her suite, uttering whatever comforting words I could think of, such as,
'Honey, everything going to turn out for the best in the
end,' and other meaningless words of that nature.

"She'd say, 'Oh I'm quite sure of that, brother. As
it is, I got everything but him off my mind.'

"I want to tell you it was the saddest thing in the
world to see; it made me sorry to my heart to witness
the way she was running down.

"One night toward the beginning of Spring—
Winter was still there but only around the edges—the
course of my nightly guard duties having carried me to
the roof, I discovered Miss Brindle up there, looking
off into the distance to as far as she could see, wind
from the river whipping at her gown.

"That was the night when she must have caught
her final chill. Well, I helped her down and she was
feverish; I made particular note of the fact that the
heat of her body came right through that shawl and
touched my hand. That's how intense it was. The

elevator was working that night and I took her down, led her to her room. I opened the door and when she saw to where I had brought her, she said, 'I realize there isn't any way in this world I can go on being without him,' says.

"Children, you can imagine the condition of my heart at that minute and I could not think of word number one to say to her; but I helped her the best way I knew how and covered her good when she lay down on that pretty little couch of hers.

"Then Miss Crystal looked up at me and she simply said, How can I stay here when all I got is gone? Death is the nearest route for me, that's all I know,' she says, and it was really heartfelt.

"Well, so I returned to the guardroom and called Stack Purdy on the intercom; Stack says, 'Phone the doctor and I will be right there.'

"Bustle? Action? I'll tell the world there was, and after the doctor a nurse came too. Lance was pacing the corridor, he looked stricken to the heart. Josea Boutwell was at his side. Lance looked me over, he looked at the new stripes on my sleeve; dear old Lance, he always had a word for me. Scarcely ever see you anymore, brother, he says to me. Right then and there and with so much on his mind, but that is just the kind of man he was.

"It went on for three more days and nights, death pursuing poor Crystal; death would not turn go of her, it seemed. Once every so often Doctor would let Lance in. What passed between those two we shall never know. Doctor wanted to take Miss B away to

Harlem Hospital but she would not be moved, says, 'This is my last home and here I stay, where I know I shall be treated right.'

"Lance looked to the doctor for guidance, for advice on what to do, and the doctor's face said *Too late*. You could see it written there; yes, it was all too plain.

"Lance says, Crystal dear, he says, no one's taking you away from here and that's my promise.

"Or words to that effect is what the nurse said he said and that is all I know. Dear old Lance. He always knew how to carry himself; he never knew what it was to be mean, tight, and tricky. Didn't know the meaning of the words, in my opinion.

"Rumor got out that Miss Brindle's last days had arrived, and in the streets of Harlem you would have heard all kinds of expressions of sympathy and sorrow. Particularly the men; they would come up to you and say, 'Poor soul lost everything she ever had,' and 'Crystal had a hell-hound on her trail since the night she landed here, poor girl.'

"Some of the ladies were tight and mean and said things like, 'Well, I do hope her sins don't rise up in front of her.'

"Oh but that was rare, children, and mostly you would have found kind words on the lips of most. Even Miss Brune got off of Crystal's back at the last and took to singing the saddest songs it has ever been my privilege to hear. My they were affecting. There was not a dry eye in the house when she gave voice to such numbers as *Look me over, baby, the last you'll see of me.* Not to mention *Come down Death right easy, easy, easy.*

"Children, oh it is hard to see a gay young girl go. Death was overtaking her; we all knew it. But who can admit a thing like that? Harlem's first anniversary was coming up and flags and pennants and all kinds of decorations were being put in place. The colors were festive but our hearts were aching, I mean they really were aching.

"Out in Harlem Plaza they were putting up the grandstand for the visiting dignitaries who would be coming up from far and wide for the festivities. Fore-man said to the carpenters, 'Gentlemen, use your soft-est hammers and I do not have to tell you why.' They did their best.

"Miss Brindle was as comfortable as could be expected. Ofttimes during the night I'd linger at her door, and the night before she went I heard her voice. Says to the nurse, says, 'Honey, kindly put some cracked ice on my head.' I was relieved; maybe she was slowly dying but she wasn't dead yet.

"Next day she sent for Stack and me, for Stack and yours truly only; well, we knew the reason why: we had shared Art Rustram's danger and it was as simple as that. I could see that Stack's heart was over-flowing; so was mine. I felt cold and chill. I had been in that room ever so many times but this time it seemed to me as if I had never been there before. It was my first view of a death bed and that made all the difference in the world, let me tell you it did.

"Stack and I we stood by her side. 'Sit down,

friends,' Miss Brinkle says, 'for I would like to see your faces one more time.'

"We did so and she raised a smile for us. It was strange. I mean she had all her color back and I thought she had it made, the worst over, and she was hooked on life again. But it was not the case; she died that night and her last words to us were these:

" 'Please don't blame me, boys,' she said.

" 'Nothing to blame you *for*, sis,' Stack simply replied.

"Miss Brindle said, 'It's just that it takes a long long time to wear someone off your mind and how can I stay here when all I got is gone?'

"I was torn up by this time. You can imagine. I had to tell myself, Now stand it like a man. I closed my eyes; I said, Go way, Death; come in, Doctor; this girl's not ready to go. I told you once, you have been told. That is what I said.

"Miss Brindle said, 'If he came back, I would not do a thing he did not like.'

"Well, she can't be held accountable for that; her mind was wandering something awful. The nurse told us we had to go. Stack took her hand and kissed it, and I did too. I mean we loved her so.

"Well, I walked to the end of the hall; Stack Purdy he went in the other direction. I was standing at a window, I looked out and saw the men; they were preparing for our first anniversary. There was such an awful pain around my heart.

"That evening was farewell time and all the lads went in to see her, that dear old crowd: Ahearn

Tucker, Jim Hardison, Josea Boutwell, Tom Bigbee, Dan Turner, names known to you from the annals of our history. It was one of the most memorable occasions I was ever present at.

"What else can I say? In the morning she was gone, that great beauty, that gay young girl; and Lance was at her side. He folded her dying arms and said his last goodbye."

"Oh my," Ngomo said.

"Yes, honey, it's sad but we all got to pay that debt someday," the old gentleman said and fell silent.

Ahmed said, "I suppose Lance mourned for her."

"Lance? Honey, the whole country mourned for her but Lance most of all. I see what you mean, honey, and I don't blame you; I was young and made the same mistake myself. It was for Lance's love that Miss Brindle pined away and died. What she wanted he did not have to give, for he had already bestowed it on us. And that is why Lance mourned her so. Oh he was beyond consoling. I mean he was really in a study from the day she died right on up to the anniversary of Harlem's first year.

"And when that great day came he put on a public face for the occasion. All of us marvelled at it for we knew how much sorrow was in him. I'm giving you the natural facts now, children. Lance's sorrow was of the greatest and do you know why? It was because he knew he had betrayed her.

"How do I know? Lance told me so, said to me one day soon after the poor girl's death, said, Brother, let me tell you something about the citizens of this great country of ours: if any one of them makes a demand, it has got to be met. And do you know why? I'll tell you why, brother, he says. It is because they would not make the demand unless it was for something they could not live without.

"His very words, children, and I knew to what he alluded. It was Miss Brindle he had on his mind, no doubt about that. He always put things in a political way, you know—well, that's how politicians are—but it was the subject of love he was talking about, I mean really talking about."

THIRTEEN

Are you with me? Then stop fooling around and listen
for I am about to tell you the tale of the last day of
Harlem's first year. Trust my word, I'm giving you the
natural facts and you won't get them anywhere else.
All right then, no monkeying around!

"Well then, here's how it was. On that fateful
morning I was up with the dew. Winter had said goodbye but it was chill enough for anybody's health, let
me tell you. I looked out the window and what did I
see? A fog was laying on the ground; it came on like
smoke; no, it wasn't good.

"And the grandstand looked all chill and wet.
What they call the bunting was up and in place all
over the town, it was many colored; and also the flags
of every friendly nation in the world. By that time the
number was considerable. Those fancy decorations
were in a sad condition due to the weather outside; I
mean they were really dragging. I hoped for sunshine;

I prayed for a pretty day; we deserved it and I wanted it for Lance's sake.

"But if I had only known, if I had only known I'd have prayed otherwise. I should have said: Lord, stop sunrise and let this day never come, is what I should have said. Well, how was I to know? That time of day the little birds began to sing and I ought to have listened and read the message right, for the message read as follows: *You will call him and he'll be gone*, that's what the little birds were saying.

"Superstition! It's a feeling I do despise but I have to admit that foreboding came over me first thing that fateful day, bang! Right off the reel. I looked out the window and down at that grandstand, saw the flags dragging and the bunting all bedraggled—no wind at all—and I said to myself: Bad luck is waiting there.

"I put the feeling down; yes, children, I put it down. What else could I do? And with an aching heart I went about my duties, checking on security. We had men every whichawhere, mingling with the citizens on the Plaza, behind the grandstand, also at windows and on the rooftops. We did not leave stone number one unturned, for a feeling was afoot that if anyone was going to make his play, this would be the day. Their opportunity and our peril, as Stack Purdy rightly phrased it.

"We did all we could, that's all I know. If you want to know about slip-ups, don't ask me because I don't know. It was the baddest luck in the world's entire history and we never did catch the man who did it; but there is one thing I'm sure of and that is this: his soul's in hell.

"Now don't rush me now, honey. It's still early morning and the fog is lying on the ground. We're not up to the terrible part yet. Let me put it off a while, honey, for my heart's not as strong as it used to be.

"I'm by the window now, fastening on my side-arm, which I was privileged to wear, being a sergeant as I believe I have told you. Checked my buttons. Squared my shoulders. Says to myself: Be a man! And I rid myself of all bad feelings by putting my mind to my duties. Said to myself: Up here in this North there is always some kind of false bad news.

"I personally checked every post we had, climbed up to every roof and down again. That kind of action had no effect whatsoever on my wind, not in those days. Up on the rooftops the boys were drinking coffee, all those corporals, privates, and PFCs, dearest friends I ever had. All gone now. Some went at the time of the invasion, left themselves on Fifth Avenue near 98th or rushing the mortars in the corn fields of Central Park; others died natural deaths, more or less recently some of them.

"Said to them all, to each and every one, 'Gentlemen,' I says, 'on your toes today and that's an order! Eyes wide open and give the double check to any unauthorized movement whatsoever.'

"At noontime exactly the sun came out, right on the dot; and your eyes would have been dazzled by the color: all that bunting, all those flags. It was really festive. The sad memory of Miss Brindle was still in our minds, it was fresh all right, but pride would not be put down and neither would jubilation. The citizenry was out in the streets and they must have numbered up in the millions. People were shaking hands all over the place, saying things like, 'Well, brother, here it is Year Two, and did you ever think we'd make it?'

"I have never in this world seen enthusiasm like it. When it comes to real enthusiasm, children, a little new country just can't be beat. It'll take the cake everytime. I mean, we were the cat's whiskers and every living soul knew it.

"Sun came out, fog went, and for my particular use—as a sergeant in the security work—it couldn't have been better. I mean the air was clear and anyone who wanted to play bad couldn't count on the right conditions for slinking, slithering and hiding himself from the sight of anyone. I was happy to see it and took it as a good sign. Said to myself, said, Never mind what you thought the little birds were saying!

"Oh my, I'm putting it off, I'm just putting it off by degrees. Well, honey, sooner or later I got to get to it, don't I? Please forgive this weak old man, dearies.

"Delegations started to arriving, first-row seats being given to representatives from the old country. They were wearing their prettiest robes, hats, and turbans; yes, it was stunning, the picture they made. And behind them were the diplomats wearing plain black suits, but they were welcome too.

"Festivities commenced with the march-past of the militia and my they were smart. They came down 125th Street like a flight of angels, not a false step, no,

not one. Oh they were beautiful. The band was playing; they got the slite of it and how they went! I mean
it really wailed. There wasn't a dry eye in the house,
let me tell you, when they belted forth those pretty old
songs. When it comes to pure sound, that band can not
be beat. It is tops.

"Jim Hardison was at the mike as usual making
the introductions. Old Jim, he knew the first name as
well as the last of every visiting dignitary. Lance said
to him once, said, Jim, should we ever have a postal
system I intend to make you first Postmaster General.
It raised a hearty laugh all around for Jim really
wasn't that type of man at all.

"He was up there at the microphone, enjoying it
to the hilt, saying, 'I now have the great privilege and
pleasure of presenting His Excellency the Ambassador
of Dahomey.' Et cetera. People from all those dear old
countries.

"There was a few preliminaries before Lance
came on. The citizens were respectful, you know, but
only gave those people half their minds. Everyone was
waiting for the main event. Lance was untouchable
when it came to occasions such as that.

"Finally—I'm getting to it now—finally Lance
stepped up to the mike, and the uproar which followed
was really something and it has never been matched.
You had to be there, honey, for I am nowhere near
up to describing it. It went past the place of descrip-
tion anyway. It was nothing more nor less than solid
pride and joy, for Lance was our own, he really was,
no doubt about it, he was our selfs.

"Oh Lord. I watched him lift his arms up to the citizens, I heard him say, Brothers and sisters, we have come through! We have made it, and now I think we have got it made for good and all!

"Those were his very words and the general joy was such that he had to repeat it three times. Lance went into the whole one-year history of Harlem, he gave a review, he told the world why we are here. He wasn't talking to *us* and the citizens knew it. They kept shouting every so often, 'Explain it to them, Lance baby!'

"And Lance he did just that; that is precisely what he did. He laid out the natural facts for all to see and there wasn't any two ways about it. We're here because we're here, he says, and what are you going to do about it? We're here because we're here and giving notice here and now that we are here to stay. Staying is everything, Lance went on, and staying is nowhere, because we are advancing into time's future, and with our feet firmly planted in this *place:* right here where we now stand!

"I tell you, children, the citizens went wild. Lance always had that way of saying deep things in a sweet and lovely way. No, he never went in for any of that fancy ta-doo stuff; he cut right to the bone every time.

"I never shall forget how he looked at that moment, so young and tall, gazing out at our new sweet land which was all our own. He waited for the sound of joy to dim down a little; and it turned out, children, it turned out that dear old Lance waited forever.

When he went down he went down with that sound in his head; and it must be so, that he is still hearing it and nothing but.

"Yes, honey, I heard the shot and I can hear it still. Oh it was dirty, oh it was a bad work, it cut off my happy days to hear it. The shot rang out and Stack threw himself in front of Lance, but it was too late, too late, too late.

"The bullet entered into Lance's breast and in a minute blood was running down. I was there beside him and I saw it; it's a wonder I'm not dead. He was so good and kind to me and I loved him clean through. Cry if you want to, honey; I don't blame you, do the same thing if I could.

"It was just about three o'clock when it happened; the bullet struck him, he reeled and fell down. He said his last goodbye and I knew by the expression on his face that he was dead.

"Well, you can imagine. In a minute all those joyous people became pilgrims of sorrow. Josea Boutwell folded Lance's arms and he then took up the reins of government, as they are called, being next in line.

"Bandmaster muffled his drums. You should have heard them roll; it was powerful and it was slow, oh my.

"But Josea picked up the beat. He walked up to the mike, sorrow all over his face, says, Children, we have come through and we are going on! We're pushing forward now, right through freedom and on to the other side!

"Honey, don't you cry that way, there is no

cause. Here it is almost three-fourths of a century later and Harlem is still casting a shadow. Like yours truly. Our little country is in the same shape that I am in at the present time and as you know I have the very best of health and nothing but good clothes, and my heart don't bother me just a little at times."

The old gentleman looked at his watch. "It's way past your bedtimes," he said. "It's late all right, but I have finished my run, brought you up to date on Harlem's first year, and you know how it has gone ever after on. We're still separate, we are still making our own history and our own arts, all seven. We have gone through the worst feelings men have ever had. When Lance went I suffered for a solid year with the poor man's heart disease; but here I am in Harlem and I'm doing very well; and as dear old Lance said that time to Mister Eddie: It is magnificent to be here!"

ABOUT
THE
AUTHOR

Warren Miller is the author of *The Cool World,* about which James Baldwin said, "One of the finest novels about Harlem that has ever come my way"; *Looking for the General,* about which Eugene Burdick said, "I really think it deserves the Pulitzer Prize"; *The Way We Live Now, Flush Times* and other books. His stories, articles and reviews have appeared in *The New Yorker, The Saturday Evening Post, Harper's Bazaar,* and elsewhere.